KU-443-609

ISLAND OF MISTS

Arasay — remote Scottish island, wildlife haven, and home to Jenna's ancestors. When she arrives to help out her great aunt in the bookshop, she's running from her past and hiding from the world. But she's not expecting to meet an attractive wildlife photographer who is also using the island to escape from previous traumas. As Jenna embraces island life and becomes closer to Jake and his family, there are secrets in the mist that could threaten their future happiness . . .

LIBRARIES NI
WITHDRAWN FROM STOCK

EVELYN ORANGE

ISLAND OF MISTS

Complete and Unabridged

LINFORD
Leicester

First published in Great Britain in 2020

First Linford Edition
published 2021

Copyright © 2020 by DC Thomson & Co. Ltd.,
and Evelyn Orange
All rights reserved

A catalogue record for this book is available
from the British Library.

ISBN 978–1–4448–4703–1

Published by
Ulverscroft Limited
Anstey, Leicestershire

Set by Words & Graphics Ltd.
Anstey, Leicestershire
Printed and bound in Great Britain by
TJ Books Ltd., Padstow, Cornwall

This book is printed on acid-free paper

1

Jenna's heart felt as if it was going to burst out of her chest as she ran along the pier. The large wheeled suitcase which she was bumping over the planks of wood behind her threatened to pull her arm out of its socket. The last car had already embarked on the ferry, and the crew were preparing to raise the ramp.

'No! Wait!' The breath was ragged in her throat, her voice feeble. To her relief, one of the crew spied her and raised a hand in acknowledgement. He waved her forward with a grin, clearly amused by her hot face and gasping breath.

'Cut it fine, didn't ye, lass?'

At last the car deck was beneath her feet, her legs trembling as she stumbled towards the stairs. 'Thank you so much!' was all she could utter,

1

exhaustion hitting her like a blow. Under her breath she grumbled about her brother and his so-called helpful idea of getting his friend to drive her from Glasgow to Oban. If she'd known that Paul's clapped out old van would get a puncture while still an hour's drive from their destination, she would have taken the train the full distance.

Jenna staggered up the stairs and deposited her suitcase in the luggage area before continuing up to the next deck to look for a place to collapse. Shouts from the crew and the noisy juddering of the engine competed with the roaring of the wind as the ferry left its moorings.

It wasn't until she reached the lounge area that she realised that her phone was buzzing in her pocket, and she reached for it wearily. On the screen was her brother Leo's name. Her fingers were still shaking with adrenaline as she touched the phone to answer his call.

'Jenna! Did you make it? Paul texted

me what happened. Are you all right?'

'Hi, yes, I'm just on board. Seeing as this is the last ferry to Arasay for days, I'm glad I didn't have to start looking for somewhere to stay in Oban. It's all been such a rush, and Aunt Morag needs me. I wouldn't have liked to let her down.'

'Sorry, that was a mistake lumbering you with Paul. But when I heard he was going up to Oban to visit his friends, I thought it more convenient than humping your suitcase on the train. I know how much stuff you like to take with you!'

Jenna smiled wryly to herself. It was true, as a child she had been renowned for packing holiday suitcases to bursting. 'This is different, Leo. I only had two days' notice, and just packed the one suitcase. Mum's going to send on more of my stuff — though I wish I could have my piano.'

'Well, why not buy a new one online and have it delivered? Get a digital one, and you won't have to worry about getting it tuned.'

She smiled. 'You know, Leo, you sometimes do have some very good ideas. Though I don't know how long Aunt Morag will need me. Still, I've packed my flute and some of the music I was learning years ago at university.' She pushed open the door of the lounge with her free hand, and caught sight of her reflection in the glass. It made her blink and start. She hadn't got used to her hair like this. As soon as she had agreed to come to Scotland, she'd impulsively had her hair cut very short, with a longer tousled fringe. Gone were the scarlet curls she had sported for the last six years or so, and her hair was now just a shade lighter than its natural mid-blonde.

'You forgive me, then?' Leo's voice in her ear brought her back to the present.

'Of course I do.' She knew he cared about her, and wished he wasn't so far away. 'Gotta go now. Love you, Leo. Bye.'

Jenna had barely disconnected the

call when a thump on her shoulder sent her phone flying through the air. Exclaiming in dismay, she whirled round to see what had hit her.

'I'm so sorry, let me get that.' A tall male figure was bending down to retrieve the phone. When he straightened up he reached around six feet tall, towering over her five feet three. His attention was on her phone in his hands, not on her, and Jenna found her indignation evaporating somehow as she watched him, mesmerised. His hair was a riot of brown waves, giving him a wild, rugged look. A shadow of reddish beard graced his chin, and the eyes beneath his lowered brows could only said to be autumn bracken in colour.

Autumn bracken! Where had that come from? She shook her head quickly and held out her hand. 'Is it all right?'

'It seems to be. I must apologise again. I was concentrating too hard on getting this through the doorway, and didn't see you.' He waved a long rangy hand at the unwieldy square case that he had now dumped at his feet. Everything about him shouted 'outdoors', from the broad shoulders under a well-worn green waterproof to his leather hiking boots. Jenna surmised that the multiple pockets on his trousers were not for fashionable show, but were utility wear for every day. His deep voice had a pleasant Scottish accent.

Suddenly Jenna realised that she was staring at him, and reached for her phone. 'It's just as well I'd finished my call.' A flush crept up under her scarf at his intent gaze, but she hoped it wasn't a look of recognition. That was the last thing she wanted. To hide her discomfort, she checked her phone. 'Yes, it seems to be OK.'

'I'm glad. Do you want me to give you my number in case I need to pay for a repair?'

Was he trying to pick her up? 'No thanks. I'll let you get on.' She didn't want to have a conversation right now. Swinging her small rucksack off her shoulder, she slipped the phone into her pocket and walked over to a seat near the window. She made a great show of opening her rucksack and looking for the paperback she'd stuffed into it at the last minute. After a minute or two of reading, she raised her eyes warily and looked round the lounge. Good — he had gone.

The initial clanking of the car ferry had changed to a constant hum now that the vessel had reversed out of its berth and was chugging along the channel between some small islands on the way to the open sea. Jenna held no illusions about what was to follow for the next ninety minutes. The wind was high, and darkness was falling. It wasn't going to be the most comfortable of crossings to the little island of Arasay.

There were only a few passengers in this area. She doubted if there were many more in the lounge on the deck above this one, and it was unlikely that anyone was on the open deck. The car deck held only five or six vans and SUVs when she had made her undignified embarkation.

Jenna purchased a coffee and a cereal bar at the cafeteria to keep her going. She knew that she would feel more settled with something inside her, especially once the ferry had left the shelter of the channel and was in the full force of the swell out on the open sea.

After about twenty minutes, rain began lashing the windows of the lounge while the deck beneath her began to roll. Her mind slipped back to the events that had brought her on this mad venture. It was just two days since she had answered the telephone at her parents' house on the coast of Northumberland.

'Is that Mrs Davidson?' a woman with a Scottish accent had asked tentatively.

'No, I'm afraid she's at work. I'm her daughter, Jenna.'

'Would you get her to ring me when

she comes home? I'm Isobel McPherson, a friend of her Aunt Morag. She's had a fall and broken both her wrists, and needs help when she comes out of hospital. I can do a bit but I have a full-time job. I've tried ringing her nephew but he says all of his family are tied up with work.' The woman sounded quite flustered.

'I'm sorry, but my mother also works full-time as a teacher, so it's not possible for her to get time off.'

The caller sighed with what sounded like despair. 'I was hoping one of her family could come and help out. The bookshop is due to go on to summer opening hours.' The caller then explained more about Aunt Morag's accident.

During this tale, Jenna had closed her eyes, her thoughts roaming to the distant Scottish island where her great aunt lived, and her mother Shona had grown up. It was a place Jenna hadn't visited since she was a child. Memories bathed in sunshine and laughter crowded into her mind, scenes of childhood holidays and fun. It was another world.

'Mum will be home in about an hour, and we'll discuss what can be done. What's your telephone number?' She scribbled it down and took more details of Aunt Morag's mishap.

Morag was a much younger sister of Jenna's grandfather. She was in fact only ten years older than her niece Shona, and at the age of sixty-four she was still running the bookshop on the island off the west coast. Morag had set up the store with her husband, and she'd continued to run it after his death three years earlier. Two weeks previously she had tripped on her step and fallen awkwardly. Because she lived alone and was unable to use her hands, she had been taken into hospital on the mainland. Now she was being allowed home, but obviously needed help. As Easter was approaching, the bookshop was due to go on to its summer schedule to cater for the tourists. To make matters worse, her part-time assistant, Caitlin, was expecting a baby within the month, but rising blood pressure had meant that she'd been advised to go and stay with her sister-in-law on the mainland in case an emergency delivery was needed.

Jenna explained all this to her bewildered mother as they prepared the dinner together.

'And Isobel definitely tried everyone else — your Uncle Duncan and Aunt Jackie, and their three?'

'Yes, but they all pleaded work. As Uncle Duncan's a vet, he couldn't take time off.'

Shona attacked the cooked potatoes with the masher. 'Your Aunt Jackie could take a few weeks off, as she could get someone else to fill in on reception.' Mulling over the problem was making her Scots accent more pronounced. 'Anyway, it's not the sort of thing that a man could do, if Morag needs help with dressing and such.' She tipped the mashed potatoes into a dish, and wiped her hand across her brow with a troubled expression.

'I could go.' Jenna felt momentarily light-headed as the implications of her words sank in.

'I wouldn't expect you to, Jenna.' Her mother looked up sharply. 'You're still recovering.'

The younger woman looked out of the window, trying to focus her thoughts as she gazed at the blue sky reflected in the sea. A brisk wind was stirring up white horses on the surface of the water. It had been a blessed relief to escape here to Northumberland to recover when she had been barely able to put one foot in front of another.

'I've recovered physically, and I know I have to leave my old life behind. That job at the charity housing project was a start, but I need to make a new start on my own. This will be a good way of getting back into the world, and I can help Aunt Morag at the same time.' Her voice sounded stronger than it had done for many months.

Her mother gave her a long look,

then hugged her. 'You know what, Jenna, I think Arasay will be the right step for you. You won't be worrying about people recognising you, and you can just be yourself. I'm sure you'll get on with Morag. I'm just sorry that I couldn't go myself, as I should have been back there years ago.'

So it was that Jenna now looked out on a different sea, wild and forbidding, buffeting the sturdy vessel as it ploughed through the darkness towards her new home.

A light somewhere ahead through the darkness caught Jenna's eye. They must be nearing Arasay and its ferry port of Tarasaig. She stood up and went to peer from the window through the sheeting rain. She could hear the wind howling round the ship. She'd heard stories of ferries circling for hours because the conditions were too stormy to dock. What if they couldn't land?

2

The light was becoming brighter as the ferry headed towards it. As Jenna moved back towards her seat, the vessel gave a lurch and she staggered. To her surprise, she found her arm gripped by a strong hand.

'All right? You nearly went over, there.'

Jenna's looked up into the concerned face of the man who had knocked her phone out of her hand earlier. 'I'm fine, thanks. Just so long as we get into Tarasaig, and don't end up stuck outside the port for hours.'

'It's been some crossing — but we would have turned back before now if there was any doubt about landing.' He sat down a couple of seats away from her. 'Is this your first trip to Arasay? If so, it's not a good introduction.' A smile hovered on his lips, crinkling his eyes with feathered creases born from hours in the outdoors.

Jenna found herself charmed, though she hadn't wanted to engage in conversation with any strangers. 'No, my mother comes from Arasay, and we used to visit once a year when I was a child. But I haven't been for many years.'

'Not many would return in March, after being used to visiting in the summer,' he said, grinning.

She shrugged. 'It was necessary. Aunt Morag has broken her wrists and needs help, and I was available, so agreed to come.'

'Not Morag Buchanan? I'm sorry to hear that. Please give her my best wishes. I'm Jake Redman, by the way.' He offered her a tanned hand. His grip was firm but surprisingly gentle.

'Jenna Davidson,' she replied, strangely reluctant to let his hand go. She made a show of putting her book back into her rucksack to hide her confusion.

At that moment the undulating of the deck decreased dramatically. 'Ah, we're entering the bay now.' An announcement came over the loudspeaker to say that drivers of vehicles should return to their cars.

'I'd better manhandle this down below,' he muttered, lifting the heavy box. Then he turned back to her. 'I noticed you embarked on foot — is someone meeting you at the pier?'

'No, I've got the taxi number in my phone. I'm going to ring as soon as we land.'

'Can I offer you a lift? It's just my old Land Rover, but I'm passing Balloch on my way home.'

Jenna's hesitation was only momentary. 'Thanks, that would be great. My suitcase is in the luggage area down below.'

Putting on their coats, they followed the other sparse contingent of passengers down the steep steps to the vehicle area. Jake stowed his box in the boot of the Land Rover then made light work of her large suitcase, for which Jenna was very glad as her arm muscles were still screaming with the effort of boarding the ferry. Briefly she mused she'd need to improve her fitness, before she slipped into the passenger seat of the Rover.

Jake hurriedly pushed papers and a used coffee cup into the back, apologising for the mess. 'I hope it doesn't smell too rank. I spend a lot of time working in this, and too little time cleaning it out.'

She was about to ask what his work was, when a screeching of metal announced that the ramp at the front of the ferry was beginning its descent. Through the gaps at each side, Jenna could see the surf frothing against the concrete ramp. Conversation was halted as they watched in fascination at the skilful manoeuvring of the captain, lining up the ramp and edging in until it was close enough to disembark cars and passengers. There were no other foot passengers. As they mounted the heaving ramp, she was glad that she hadn't had to face the elements without the protection of the Land Rover. The crew member who had welcomed her on board waved at her and grinned as they passed. He was probably glad that he hadn't had to help her get the suitcase up the ramp, which was skipping alarmingly at each surge of the waves.

Jake's Land Rover was the last vehicle to disembark, and with a salute to the crew supervising the operation, he drove down the floodlit pier. They plunged into the unlit route that led from the port. It should have looked completely black, but the horizontal rain was illuminated by the headlights, offering glimpses of bushes and trees at the sides of the single-track road which circled the small island.

Jenna wanted to ask Jake about himself, but didn't relish having the sort of conversation where they exchanged information about their lives. She preferred just to be known as

Morag's great niece. Her companion seemed to be lost in his own thoughts. But just when the silence between them began to feel uncomfortable, he began to speak.

'It's not a very nice welcome for you on your return to Arasay.' He had to raise his voice so that she could hear him over the drumming of the rain on the roof of the car. 'Have you ever seen it like this before?'

Jenna gave a brief laugh, which corresponded to a bump in the road, and it came out louder than she had intended. 'No, I'm certainly seeing a different side of it. We usually came at the end of May, and I remember having lovely weather. But we haven't been for years, as my grandparents are both dead.'

He turned his head briefly to her, then pulled his gaze immediately back to the road. 'So your mother hasn't been back either?'

'I thought it would be the talk of Arasay, that Shona McCrinan didn't see her father again after he remarried.'

A flash of his white teeth reflected in the light from the headlamps. 'Well, maybe it was, but I've not been one for gossip, myself. Plus, I work away. I'm just back from a trip to Canada.'

'That sounds marvellous. I've always wanted to visit there.' Before she could ask him why he'd been there, the first houses of Balloch, the main village of Arasay, came into view. 'That's the road to Aunt Morag's. It's the house with the bookshop attached.'

'It's a great little shop. I'm so glad that your aunt kept it on after her husband died.'

'Yes, he died far too young.'

Jake suddenly stamped on the brakes, and only the swift locking of the seatbelt prevented her from being thrown forward. She exclaimed.

'Sorry, are you all right?' He barely waited for her nod of assent before he was unbuckling his own belt and opening the door, letting in a rush of wind and rain. He raised his voice over the weather. 'There's someone lying at the side of the road — look, over there!'

Peering through the rain, Jenna thought that she could see a shape half in the ditch at the roadside. Jake leapt out of the Land Rover and slammed the door shut. She watched as he loped over to the shape and bent over. As he did so, she began to make out a leg and an arm, the pale hand outlined by the headlights of the vehicle. Her heart was pounding, her breath tight as shock gripped her body. The person looked limp and lifeless. Being there on such a night didn't bode well.

Jake strode back towards her, the headlamps illuminating the grim planes of his face. He only glanced at her briefly as he rummaged in the pocket of his waterproof for his phone. He gave an exclamation of impatience. 'No signal. Do you have one on your phone?'

With trembling fingers she took out her phone and checked. 'No, there's nothing.'

'We'll take the Rover a bit further up the hill, as there should be enough signal there.' He climbed back in and released the handbrake.

'Should I wait with the person?'

He shook his head grimly. 'I'm afraid it's too late for him. I couldn't find any signs of life.' He slipped his phone into her hand. 'Let me know as soon as a signal appears.'

Jenna's mind felt numb as the Land Rover bounced up the track. They were almost at Morag's house before she called out, 'There's a signal now!'

Thanking her, he stopped the vehicle and took the phone, stepping outside to make his call. She couldn't hear what he was saying over the noise of the rain and the windscreen wipers. His call was brief. Soon he was back beside her.

'I'll drop you off. I think it would be better if you didn't say anything about this to your aunt, or anyone else, for the moment. The police will be along directly. I'm really sorry — do you think you can put it from your mind?'

'I'll try. Do you know the man?'

Jake shook his head. 'He's a stranger to me. Maybe the police will have some idea. Come on, let's get you into the warm and dry.'

It only took a few seconds to reach Morag's house. There was a light on at the door, and a glow showing behind the curtains of the front room. 'I'll get your case from the back.'

Jenna hopped out of the vehicle, slinging her rucksack over one shoulder and hurrying to the door, where she rapped sharply on the wood. Jake came up behind her and dumped the case beside her. 'I'd better get back down the track and wait for the police. Hopefully they won't need me for long, as my family will be expecting me, and I don't want them to worry. Please give your aunt my very best wishes.'

'I will, thank you. It was very kind of you to bring me.' A slight sinking sensation caught her as he hurried back to jump into the driver's seat. Somehow she didn't want him to go, but something told her that she hadn't seen the last of Jake Redman.

Then a rattle of bolts behind her drew her attention and she swung round. She was greeted by a woman with shoulder-length dark hair who appeared to be in her forties.

'Come in! We're so glad you're here safely. What a night. Are you soaked? 'The woman's eyes were dancing with warmth.

Feeling as if she was being swept in on a gust of words as well as the elements outside, Jenna found herself in a small hallway with a rack of coat hooks.

'There, let me take your coat. I see you got a lift? That was lucky.' The woman shook Jenna's waterproof with a quick flick, then dumped it on the end hook. 'Now, give me your suitcase. I'll take it upstairs if you want to go in and say hello to your auntie.' She dropped her voice to a whisper. 'She just came home yesterday evening, and she's a bit tired. You will be too, so I'm looking after you this evening.'

Jenna pushed open the door and stepped into the place that was to be her home for the next few weeks. Her strange experience with Jake receded as she stepped into her new life. A woman with dark hair only slightly streaked with grey was sitting in one of the armchairs that flanked the open fire. Her face was turned towards the door, eyebrows raised, and mouth set tensely. Her left arm was in a cast and resting in a sling, the other hand protected by a wrist guard.

Jenna dropped her rucksack on to the nearest chair and hurried forward. 'Aunt Morag! How are you?' There was only a vague recollection of this person she hadn't seen since her childhood.

At her words, the uncertain expression left her great aunt's face, and she relaxed into a smile, holding out her right arm tentatively. 'Jenna, how kind of you to come all this way to lend me a hand. I'm sorry to be such a nuisance to the family.' Her eyes brimmed with unshed tears.

A pang of sympathy caught Jenna. 'It was the least I could do.' She leaned in and carefully hugged the older woman, taking care not to jar the hands. 'You mustn't worry about causing inconvenience. I was available, and I must confess it's a bit of an adventure for me, coming back to Arasay after all these years.'

Morag used the fingers of her right hand to stroke Jenna's cheek as she knelt on the floor beside the fire. 'Well, I'm so grateful. I'll do my best not to be too much of a burden, and you can get to know the island again and enjoy its peace and tranquillity. Now, you must be tired, and hungry too, I bet.'

Jenna nodded ruefully. 'I've just been snatching at food all day.' The nightmare of the dead body flashed into her mind, and she pushed it away.

As the door opened and the other woman returned, Morag looked up. 'Isobel's made us a meal, and it just needs reheating.'

Isobel hurried through towards the kitchen, calling as she did so, 'It'll be ready in ten minutes. Why don't you go upstairs, Jenna, and freshen up? Your room is the one at the back, at the end of the corridor. The bathroom's next door, and there are some towels on your bed.'

'Thanks, I will. I'll be down promptly. I've just realised that I'm ravenous — it's probably the relief at surviving the crossing.'

They all laughed, the ice broken, and within a few minutes she had returned downstairs to a plate of steaming food. Isobel reached for her coat. 'Well, I'll be off home to my husband, if you don't mind washing your dishes. I'll pop in tomorrow after school to see how you're managing and maybe take you for a drive round the island on Saturday, so that you can get your bearings.'

'That would be great, thanks.' Jenna remembered Isobel telling her on the phone that she was a schoolteacher.

They didn't wait up late. Jenna was thankful to find herself alone in her bedroom, having helped Morag get into her night clothes. Now she couldn't resist twitching back a curtain to look out of the window. The windows were still wet, but not buffeted by the wind. Beyond the house was utter blackness. It felt strange to be so far from the bustle of mainland life — but oddly comforting, cocooned in anonymity. This was the beginning of a new chapter of her life, and a spark of excitement ignited within her.

Then she blinked as a tiny light winked in the distance from the deep black of the night. Craning her head forward, she strained her eyes. Yes — there it was again, and it blinked once, twice, and then was gone. All was dark again. Shrugging, she stepped back, pulled the curtains, and climbed into bed. She didn't envy anyone being out in a night like this.

As she gave a huge yawn and pulled

up the warm quilted coverlet, she banished the nightmarish recollection of the discovery of the dead man, and instead allowed herself to think of the enigmatic, attractive companion of the last part of her journey. What a pity he was attached, she thought, then gave herself a mental ticking off. Men were off the menu — she was here to look after Aunt Morag and the bookshop, and to get used to being out in the world again. But the memory of those bracken-coloured eyes swam before her as she fell into a deep slumber.

3

It was becoming light as Jenna opened her eyes, astonished that she had slept so soundly for the first time in years. Aunt Morag had said not to get up early, that she would manage to dress herself and have some cereal if she was hungry. So Jenna allowed herself a leisurely shower before going downstairs.

That morning she familiarised herself with the house, Morag showing her where everything was kept. Midmorning Jenna made them both a hot drink, and they relaxed in the main sitting room in front of the open fire. It was a comfortable space, lined with bookshelves containing the collections of two avid readers — Morag and her husband John, who had died suddenly a few years back of a brain haemorrhage. There were many photos of the two of them together. They also had an extensive collection of recorded music.

Wondering how new Morag's collection was, Jenna leaned forward slightly, and drew in her breath sharply as she recognised the CDs on the end. 'I didn't know that you had anything by Urban Hawk — but you've got them all!'

Morag smiled. 'Yes, all three CDs. I didn't just buy them because it was your group — I really quite like the music. You're a talented girl, Jenna.'

The words felt hollow to her now. Her years in the group seemed like a dream. 'I'm finished with that, and I've got no creativity left. After all those years on the road, in the recording studios, and writing songs, I burned myself out completely. I'm only now beginning to feel that I'm over the pneumonia that I developed last year. I could never go back. Devon has never forgiven me.'

'Ah, Devon. Was he more than just your singing partner?'

Jenna closed her eyes, seeing in her mind's eye the tall, rangy guitarist with his black hair and dark eyes. His unusual husky voice had beguiled her when they met at university on their music course, and they had started vocalising together. Jenna had discovered in herself a talent for writing songs that showed off their abilities. Urban Hawk was formed, with Jenna playing the piano, Devon on electric guitar, and their friend Max on drums.

It had been almost instantaneous success. Their studies abandoned, they had embarked on a career on the road, becoming wilder each year as they sounded off each other. They had developed a gritty, urban rock sound, but with hints of folk, and it had struck a chord, literally, with their fans.

They had burned brightly for six years, and recorded three albums in that time, with a fourth in the pipeline. It had been tough for her, writing all the songs, and as her ideas began to dry up it turned into a nightmare before everything came crashing down. Jenna wrenched her attention back to the soft glow of the room, and sighed.

'I was dazzled by Devon for some time, and yes, we were involved. After a while it became habit. Latterly it was difficult. He became so controlling, dictating what sort of music I should write. I told him he could do much more. After all, he was a musician too. He never understood how much it took out of me.'

'So is the group still going without you?'

'Devon's tried going solo, though Max plays for his backing band. He's been writing some stuff, but his debut album that came out three months back hasn't been a massive success so far. He was still pestering me at home while I was recovering, wanting me to start writing again. But I can't — it's all gone.' Jenna blinked away tears of regret from her eyes. Then she lifted her chin defiantly. 'I have to reinvent myself, now. Mum and dad's home in

Northumberland was a refuge, but I need to get back out into the world, and become Jenna Davidson — not Linnet any more.'

'Linnet! That was a stroke of genius, using your middle name as your professional one.'

Jenna thought fondly of her two grandmothers, Lily Davidson and Janet McCrinan, whose names had been joined to form her second name. 'Yes, and as my real name isn't really known, it gives me a chance to be a new person now. I dyed out the scarlet hair as soon as I went back north.'

Morag nodded. 'I must say I like the new look.'

'My hair was a mess up until two days ago. This was a drastic remake. I hardly recognise myself.' Then she added tentatively, 'I've brought my flute with me. I hope you don't mind. I'll play in my room, and not if you're resting.'

'Play whenever you like. It'll be good to hear music in the house again.'

Her great aunt then suggested that Jenna should go out into the village to buy a few items. When she stepped outside, she filled her lungs with the delicious fresh air. It was a dull and drizzly day, but the soft contours of the landscape were calming. Jenna gazed at the road that ribboned for about a mile down to the sea, with a fork halfway that went towards the port.

There were rocks and a beach just visible from her vantage point. Jenna vowed to go down at the earliest opportunity. It was one of the memories she had from her childhood, running on the golden sands and exploring in the rockpools of Arasay.

Then her attention was caught by the fluttering of some blue tape further down the road, obviously set by the police last night. With a quick glance back to the house to confirm that she wasn't being observed, she hurried down the track and then branched off down the road out of the village towards the place where the dead man had lain.

It didn't take her long to reach the scene, which was deserted. It was right beside the sign for Balloch. With her finger, Jenna traced the Gaelic name at the top of the sign: Baile an Loch. She was really here, on this fascinating island! Beside the signpost was a bank covered in coarse yellowed grasses, a deep ditch, and what looked like peat bog beyond, leading towards the coast. The ground was trampled by boots, and the remnants of tape hung, shredded and discarded on their metal supports. It looked abandoned. Realising that she would discover no more, Jenna set off back towards the village centre.

Morag's bookshop and house were situated on a track which branched from the main street of the village. Jenna stopped for a moment to survey the shops and get her bearings. There was a small supermarket at the far end of the road with a car park, bustling with activity. Amongst the village stores such as the bakery, newsagent's and pharmacy, Jenna noted the usual batch of tourist outlets. When Jenna entered the baker's shop, a delicious aroma of warm bread engulfed her. The other customers were deep in discussion and didn't turn their heads.

'Who was it?' one of two women asked.

'A complete stranger, not one of us,' the shop assistant replied in a low, shocked tone. 'It must be a visitor, but I believe they're all accounted for. It's a complete mystery.'

Jenna realised that the news of the dead man must have quickly spread round Balloch. She didn't join in, not wanting to draw attention to herself. Both the women left the shop, so the assistant turned politely to Jenna, who explained that she was Morag's great-niece. The woman's expression became sympathetic, and there followed a discussion of Morag's health.

Once she had completed her shopping, Jenna sauntered down the road, looking in the shop windows. She had little recollection of Balloch from when she was a child. While she mulled over the conversation she had overheard about last night's incident, her attention was caught by a craft shop display on the opposite side of the road. Jenna crossed over and stood entranced, gazing at jewel-coloured balls of wool, tapestries, and a glorious throw knitted in an intricate design. There was also a gallery of original art on the long wall leading to the back of the shop.

Someone was pinning up a poster on the inside of the glass door. The door opened with the jingle of a bell, and a cheery round face with curly brown hair peeped round the gap. 'Hello! Would you like to come in and look round?'

Astonished, Jenna was going to decline, but the smile of the young woman enticed her in. 'Thanks — but I haven't long. My aunt's expecting me back shortly.'

'Just browse at your own leisure. I'm Rachel — just give me a shout if you want anything.' She disappeared to the back of the shop, where she picked up some knitting in a deep royal purple. Jenna followed her invitation and strolled round. It was an Aladdin's cave, filled with knitting wools, craft supplies, plus finished articles on sale. Jenna's breath was taken away at the intricacies of the tapestries on display, pieces of art with beads and gold thread mixed in the wools. There were also original paintings of the island, and carved wooden figurines.

'Lovely, aren't they? Most of our goods are by local people.' Rachel's knitting needles clicked softly as her fingers moved, as if she was hardly aware of what her hands were doing.

'Did you knit those garments on the rail?'

'Quite a few — we have a circle of knitters, and we often meet to knit in the shop for a chat and a cup of coffee. There are details on the wall if you're interested. It's for everyone who enjoys crafts — complete beginners too.' Her eyes twinkled as if she had deduced that Jenna wasn't experienced in that field.

'It's not really an option at the moment as I'm here to look after my Aunt Morag and the bookshop.'

'I heard that someone was coming to help her. Well, you'd be very welcome at our group. I know what it's like to be a stranger in a new place. We're a friendly bunch.'

Jenna smiled, recognising that the woman's accent had a Yorkshire twang. Thanking Rachel, she left the shop and turned towards the hill. The school must be out now for the day, as she noticed a couple of mothers with children, and there was a family getting into a Land Rover which had parked outside the hardware store. Her heart skipped a beat, remembering her journey with Jake the evening before. Then she told herself that half the people on the island must own similar vehicles.

A woman helped a little girl into the back seat, then climbed in behind her.

At that moment, the man who was closing the boot turned towards Jenna, and a flash of welcome recognition caught her. There was no mistaking that tall athletic figure with the unruly curls and the line of beard on his chin. His eyes locked with hers, and a current of electricity seemed to pass along their gaze. For a moment he seemed to hesitate, then he closed the tailgate. She heard him call 'back in a moment' to the others in the car, and he strode down the road towards her.

'Hello Jenna. How is your aunt — and how are you? I hope you weren't too upset by what happened last night.'

Jenna tried to appear calm and in control of her emotions. Ridiculous that she could feel so disturbed at seeing this stranger again, a man clearly with a family. 'Thank you, I'm doing okay. Aunt Morag is naturally rather tired, so I'm out getting to know the place again and shopping for a few items.' She turned her gaze back down the road. 'I saw that there was police tape round

41

the area this morning. And I overheard someone in the bakery say that the man is unknown.'

His mouth twisted wryly. 'The village tom-toms are at work already. Yes, I checked at the police station earlier this morning. No-one seems to know who the man was. They're beginning an investigation now. I hope you'll put it from your mind and not let it disturb you.'

Nodding her head, she decided that he was right. It was nothing to do with her. Then she glanced back towards the car. 'Are you enjoying being back with your family?'

Jake's eyes softened as he looked back towards the Land Rover. 'Yes, it's great to be back reading bedtime stories in person for my daughter. It's not the same on the other end of a phone.' The deep musical tone of his Scots accent was pleasant on her ears.

The subject of their conversation wound down the window and called, 'Come on, Daddy! You said we could go down to the seashore.'

He laughed. 'I'm sorry, but I'm going to have to dash off. Seven-year-olds can be very imperious! No doubt I'll see you again soon. Goodbye.'

She couldn't prevent herself from gazing after him in appreciation as he returned to the vehicle with long strides, the wind ruffling his hair. There was something compelling and almost vulnerable in his long tanned face with its hollow cheeks and serious expression, lit by his slow smile. But there was nothing vulnerable about that lean, muscular body. She wished she knew more about him. No doubt Aunt Morag would be able to fill her in. Arasay was a small enough place that he would be known, she was sure.

4

Back at the house, all thoughts of Jake Redman were pushed from Jenna's mind when Morag greeted her. 'Your mother telephoned. She said she'd tried you on your mobile, but you must have been out of range. The signal tends to dip as you go down the street — it's best on the upper floor of the house.'

Jenna looked at her mobile and found that she did indeed have a missed call. 'I'll ring her back when I've stored the shopping.'

After asking how Jenna was settling in, Shona swiftly moved on to the reason for her call. 'There's an office-franked letter arrived for you with a London postmark. Would you like me to forward it to you?'

Jenna's heart began to pound, and she gripped the telephone receiver more tightly. 'That sounds ominous. Would you open it for me now, and tell me what it says?'

There was the sound of tearing of paper as Shona found her way into the envelope. 'It's from a firm of solicitors. They're writing to inform you that Niall Devon has petitioned you for compensation on the dissolving of the group, Urban Hawk, and to sort out the copyright of all your songs. They are proposing a hearing in July, and want your solicitor to contact them.'

The phone nearly slipped from Jenna's hand as the strength drained from her whole body. 'Compensation! I was the one who wrote the songs. He's got a nerve. Devon helped a bit with the arrangements, but it was my work.'

'Are you in touch with your solicitor?'

'I haven't been for a while. The dissolving of the group was ticking along in the background. It's just like Devon to try and pre-empt me and push it into court. How dare he! I'd better contact Richard Holman straight away. Will you scan the letter and email it to me, please?'

Morag looked up from her magazine when Jenna returned to the main room. 'You look concerned — I hope there's nothing wrong.'

Sitting down, Jenna explained the situation. 'They're my songs, not Devon's!'

'That's outrageous! Your mum always said how hard you worked on the music. So what now? Will you need to go back to England?'

Jenna recognised the anxiety behind Morag's question. Quickly she reassured her. 'No, that won't be necessary, as the hearing will be later this year. I'm here for a while, don't worry.'

To calm her great aunt, Jenna picked up a photo from the shelf by the fire. It showed Morag and her husband John with Jenna's grandfather, Malcolm, and her grandmother, Janet.

'I often thought of Granny during my singing years. I was only thirteen when she died. Granny and Grandpa's house was bleak without her when we came the following May. That was my last visit. I always recall Grandpa being rather gruff and distant. It was Granny who made our holidays fun. It changed things for Mum, too, when Granny died. She never really talks about why we stopped coming.'

'Well, you know that your grandfather remarried not long after your last visit.' Jenna nodded. 'Francesca, the wicked stepmother.'

Morag gave a gulp of laughter. 'Your mother actually calls her that?'

'Not in so many words, but whenever she does mention her, I can tell that Mum dislikes her thoroughly.'

Morag nodded. 'It was tragic that your grandmother died so young — sixty-four, the same age that I am now. She'd cut her leg working in the garden, and by the time we realised how bad it was, sepsis had set in. Your grandfather blamed himself. Being a doctor, he thought he should have recognised what was happening. But

Janet was the sort of person who always got on with things, no matter what. She didn't want to cause any trouble, and thought that it would heal on its own.'
She opened a photograph album, and pointed to a photograph of Granny Janet standing in the garden with her trowel, laughing.

Jenna took the album from her and began flicking through. 'I suppose that's why Grandpa went off on a cruise the year after she died.'

'Yes, he missed her desperately, and found the house achingly empty. He was away four weeks, and no one was more surprised than I was when he returned with Francesca on his arm. They were married a few months later, and spent much of their married life away from home.'

'Did you get on with Francesca? Mum thinks she was shallow, only interested in the high life — also that she was on the lookout for someone to take care of her.'

'Yes, she was needy, but so was

Malcolm. He couldn't live without Janet, and Francesca filled part of the void. I didn't have much in common with her, but she wasn't a bad person. I'm just grateful that she made his last years less empty. Malcom didn't handle the situation with your mother very well, being the pig-headed person he always was. I told him he should have recognised Shona's grief as well, and reached out to her with understanding. But he said that she was being hysterical and melodramatic, and that it was none of her business what he did with his life.'

'I think that Mum regrets now that she didn't try harder to mend the breach in their relationship. His death came as a blow to her. I was on the road at the time, but I know that she was devastated.'

'It's been six years since he went, but I've not seen Francesca again. She married again two years ago.'

'Really?'

'You have to understand that Francesca

was a very lonely person, and needed someone to love her. She was fifty-nine when your grandfather died. Francesca had no reason to come back to Arasay, as she never liked the house.'

Jenna nodded. 'Did you never fancy living there yourself?'

Morag closed the photograph album. 'No, it's really a family home — and by the time she sold it, John had died. In any case, it suits me to live next to the bookshop.'

'I'm really looking forward to working there. When do I start?'

Her great aunt looked pleased. 'We'll go in tomorrow. We need to prepare to open again.'

The next day, Morag handed the keys to Jenna so that she could unlock the door of the little prefab building. 'In a couple of weeks it's the school Easter break, and we'll have the first visitors of the year coming to the island.'

The public area of the shop was lined with glass-fronted wooden cabinets, which gave the place the cosy feel of a personal library. There was a large wooden counter with a chair, and behind this a panel with posters of island events — a ceilidh, a Scottish dancing competition, a Tai Chi class, and an art exhibition. There were also two stands, one displaying postcards, the other greetings cards with a local theme. Morag took her through to the back of the shop.

This space was the storeroom, with a small kitchen area — a sink, some cupboards and a worktop on which sat a kettle and a microwave oven. Morag flicked a switch on an electric heater, then walked over to a pile of boxes near the back door, and studied the labels. 'This is our latest delivery. A neighbour let Ruaridh in when he brought the delivery on Tuesday.'

'Ruaridh?' Jenna raised her eyebrows.

'Yes, Ruaridh MacAllister. He's the son of the garage owner, and he runs the delivery service on the island. A nice lad, not much older than you. Lovely singing voice, too. You'll hear him perform at the next ceilidh. We have one a month in winter, more in the summer, for the visitors.' She turned back to the boxes. 'Could you open these boxes and stack the new books on these shelves here in the backroom? Give me the invoices — they should be on the top.'

The second box contained larger books. The top one caught Jenna's attention immediately.

'*Island Eye — Portrait Of Arasay And Its Wildlife*,' she read out. 'So who is the author, Jared? The name sounds familiar.'

Her face lighting up, Morag put down the invoices. 'That's our local celebrity. If you like wildlife programmes you'll probably have seen him on television. He's a wildlife cameraman and photographer. Jared's his professional name.'

When Jenna turned over the book, her breath caught in her throat. She found herself gazing at a large black and white portrait of the author with his camera — it was Jake Redman.

Morag came over to stand at Jenna's shoulder. 'Jakob Alexander Redman is his full name. I don't know who thought up the name Jared — obviously a contraction of J.A. Redman. I must ask him next time he's in here.'

Jenna looked up sharply, her heart beating faster. 'So he comes in the bookshop?'

'He always signs the copies that we keep in stock. I don't know if he's at home just now, because he's away on assignments a lot.'

'But he is here — it was Jake who gave me a lift from the ferry when I arrived.'

Jenna recalled the large hard case he was carrying on the ferry — obviously some camera equipment he didn't want to leave in his vehicle. Drawn again to the author portrait on the back of his book, she felt herself tingle. Don't be such a fool, she told herself. He's unavailable.

Jenna and Morag worked solidly

through the morning, unpacking the books. There was a chance for Jenna to get to know the stock. When it came to lunchtime, she returned to the row of books by 'Jared'.

'May I buy one of these? I'd love to read it.'

'Of course. You must telephone him and see when he wants to come in and do his signing, and he can do yours too.'

'What, now?' Jenna felt oddly flustered.

'There's a telephone book in the drawer of the counter. We're not very hi-tech here!'

Jenna made herself dial the number before she chickened out. It rang for a long time, and with relief she was about to replace the receiver when someone answered.

'Hello?' It was his voice.

Her mouth felt dry. 'Oh, hello. This is Jenna Davidson telephoning from the Arasay bookshop.' She turned away from Morag so that she wouldn't notice her shaking hand.

'Well hello, Jenna. I hope you're settling in all right. So you're working in the bookshop already?'

'Yes, we've received a delivery of your book, *Island Eye*, and I believe that you normally sign some copies for sale here.'

'That's right. Could I come after lunch?'

Jenna felt herself flush with pleasure at the thought of seeing him again. 'Yes, that would be fine. Just knock on the door when you arrive.'

When this arrangement was relayed to Morag, she nodded. 'Good, that means we'll have plenty for the start of the Easter holiday. Now, you can have your copy at cost. Do you have a bank card with you? It'll be a good opportunity for you to do a transaction.'

They went through the workings of the till, before it was finally time to return to the house for lunch. Jenna flicked through her book while she was eating her sandwiches. 'It covers a whole year on Arasay. I thought you said he was away a lot of the time.'

Morag sat beside her. 'He wrote that the year after his wife died, when he brought the little girl back to Arasay. I think they'd been living abroad somewhere. He wanted life to be settled for the wee one after she lost her mummy.'

Puzzled, Jenna looked up. 'But I saw him in the village yesterday with a woman as well as his little girl. I assumed it was his wife.'

Morag laughed. 'I don't suppose you looked very closely. That would be his mother, Ailsa. She was in the year below me at primary school. The wee girl lives with her while Jake's away.'

Jenna's heart was pounding again at the thought that Jake wasn't tied up after all, though she was sorry to hear that there had been a family tragedy. 'Yes, she was inside the car. I couldn't see her very well.' She paused, before asking, 'What happened to his wife?'

'I'm not sure — a car accident, I

think. No-one really talks about it.'

Jenna began flicking through the book, drinking in the detailed shots of birds and animals, with some sweeping views of beaches and wild places. A deep longing to explore these habitats was growing in her with every turn of the page. 'Does the bookshop have any guides to Arasay? I've brought my hiking boots with me, and I've been walking a lot over the last few months with Dad to build up my stamina.'

'Yes, that shelf over there.' Morag tilted her head and regarded her with amusement. 'I assumed you had turned into a big city girl and that you would find it the back of beyond, here.'

Jenna shook her head. 'I feel as if I'm a prisoner set free. I've really begun to enjoy being outdoors. I'm not a pop star any more — though to be honest, I don't know what I am now. I'd appreciate it if you would keep my past secret.'

'Of course. I'll just say that you're recuperating after an illness. We can be vague about what you were doing in London.' Once they had eaten lunch, Morag gave a weary sigh. 'Now, if you don't mind, I'll leave you to deal with Jakob, as I fear that my eyes are closing. Just make sure that you lock the shop when you leave.'

Jenna found herself tense and fidgety trying to concentrate on the guide books, wondering when Jake would arrive. It wasn't long before there was a tap on the outside door. Taking a deep breath, she hurried to admit Jake.

He was blown in on a gust of wind. His hair blew wildly round his face, which was illuminated by a grin. 'Thanks. It's becoming blustery out there. Where do you want me?'

Jenna tried to appear calm, though her pulse was racing. 'The box is in the back room, but maybe we should bring the books through so that you can sit at the desk to sign them.'

While he set to, she began to examine the stock of Scots novels. All the time she was conscious of the vibrant young man sitting at the desk, aware of the smell of fresh air he had brought in with him, and the strong movements of his limbs as he opened each book to sign his name.

Mesmerised, she was hardly aware that the time had sped by, and he placed the last book on the pile. 'There, all done.'

Suddenly, Jenna remembered her own copy. 'I bought one this morning — would you sign it for me as well?'

He gave her a smile that made her insides feel as if they were melting. 'Of course. Where is it?'

When Jenna placed it on the desk, he said, 'Would you like me to dedicate it to you?'

A blush stained her cheeks. 'Well, if you don't mind.' What would he write for her? She watched curiously over his shoulder.

'For Jenna, wishing you happy times on Arasay — Jared (Jakob Redman),' he wrote.

'You only signed the others as 'Jared'.'

'I sign my real name for friends,' he told her, his lips curling upwards.

'Thanks — though we don't know each other, yet.' Taking her courage in both hands, she continued, 'Maybe we could remedy that — have you time to stay for a coffee?'

'I'd love to, but I have some things to do before school finishes for the day.'

Disappointment flooded her. 'Of course. You need to be there for your daughter.'

Jake was putting his jacket back on. 'Are you going to the ceilidh on Saturday? It's the last one before the visitors begin to arrive for the season. It'll be only islanders this time, so you can meet a lot of us.' He gave a fond smile. 'I'll be bringing Talli, my little girl — she loves to dance.'

'I can't remember any Scottish dances.'

'No need to worry — you'll soon pick them up. Nobody worries if you trip over your feet, or go the wrong way. It's just good, clean fun.'

His grin won her over. 'I'll try to be there. Is it at the village hall?'

'Seven-thirty for the first dance.' Jake followed her to the door. But as he looked outside his eyes narrowed. 'What's that fellow doing at the Land Rover?' He pushed open the door with a shout. 'What do you want?' His anger was directed at a muscular man, probably aged about forty, with dark hair and a stubbly beard, who was bending down, examining the front wheel of the Rover. He sprang to his feet.

'I thought your tyre tread looked a bit thin. I'm Grant Fenton, and I work at MacAllister's garage. We could give you a good deal if you want to bring it in.' The smile on his face looked forced.

Jake stalked over to the other man and faced up to him. He was a good three or four inches taller than Fenton, and he seemed to be making the most of his advantage to intimidate him. 'I know when I need something done to the Rover, and I know Angus and Ruaridh. I'm quite capable of making the decision when it's necessary.' He gave the man a curt nod, then flung open the door of the vehicle and climbed swiftly inside. The engine sprang to life and he circled the car round. Noticing Jenna standing at the door of the shop, he gave a brief wave before driving off.

Grant Fenton turned to her. The grimace on his face looked menacing to her. Quickly she stepped back inside and locked the door. That apparently innocuous incident had clearly rattled Jake, and as a result she distrusted this man. But even this confrontation couldn't dispel the warm glow brought by spending time with Jake.

5

On Saturday morning, Isobel took Jenna for a drive round the island, so that she could become familiar with it. She arrived home sated with views of mountains, wild seascapes, remote houses, and full of excitement that they had seen several buzzards above the trees on the north side, as well as many sea birds on the shores.

'I even recognised the way down to Granny and Grandpa's house, Ballintroon. Though not much else jogged my memory,' she told Morag while preparing the bookshop counter. She noticed that her hands were trembling at the thought of dealing with customers for the first time, and realised that she had been babbling in her nervousness.

In the end they were too busy for her to remain anxious for long. When they turned the sign to 'Closed', Morag looked tired. 'Well, it was nice of everyone to call in, but I never expected us to be so busy. It's not usually like this.'

Jenna was putting the key in the lock when a shape appeared on the other side of the window, and a hand knocked on the glass.

'Am I too late?' Rachel from the craft shop burst through the door, panting with exertion. 'I was hoping I could buy a nice card, as I'd forgotten that it's a friend's birthday tomorrow, and I know I'll see her at the ceilidh tonight.'

'I'll lock the door behind you now and you can choose something.'

'Thanks — I've run all the way from my shop after closing up at five-thirty. I remembered that you were staying open later today.' She wiped a hand over her forehead as she hurried over to the cards. 'As you can see, I'm not used to such exertion — but I could do with losing a few pounds, so it won't have done me any harm.'

Jenna grinned, finding that she liked this young woman. Rachel quickly chose a card and paid for it. 'I hope you'll be at the ceilidh. It'll give you a chance to meet some more of the islanders.'

'Well, I'm not sure . . . ' Jenna was quite daunted by the prospect of entering a hall full of strangers, especially as Morag wouldn't be going.

'Rachel's right. You must go.'

'Why not come with me?' Rachel offered. 'We can sit together.'

Jenna gave in, realising there was nothing further from her old life than a traditional style Scottish ceilidh on a remote island.

At twenty past seven that evening, Jenna left the house with Rachel. 'I just put on jeans and a shirt — I hope that's suitable.'

Rachel chuckled. 'Don't worry, we don't all dress up in tartan or anything — though some of the men wear kilts, which is nice. I'm partial to a strong muscled leg and a swinging sporran.'

Their breath condensed in the cool air around them as they set off up the hill. Rachel was wearing a knee-length skirt in a warm cherry red, with black tights and ankle boots. A wide knitted scarf in hues of blue with touches of red was swathed round her shoulders. 'That's so gorgeous,' Jenna commented. 'I wish I could knit something like that — I only ever did basic knitting when I was younger, and I've forgotten how.'

'If you come along to our group you'll soon get the hang of it.'

'I'll see how things go with the bookshop.' After they reached the top of the bank and started on the path to the hall, Jenna continued, 'So how long have you been living on Arasay? I can tell you're not a native.'

For a few moments, Rachel's only reply was a burst of laughter. 'Can't hide my Yorkshire roots, even after two years! Maybe I'll sound like a Scot if I stay for the next twenty.'

Then she became serious. 'My boyfriend Will and I visited here for a holiday three years ago. We loved it — we were both in banking jobs in Sheffield, but it was like being on a treadmill. It was so peaceful here. I'd always dreamed of starting a craft shop, and I realised what a great place this was, with traditions of knitting, weaving and spinning. Will was painting in his spare time, and selling quite a few pictures.

'The craft shop was run by a very elderly lady who wanted to retire. My grandfather had died a year earlier and I decided to use my legacy as a down payment for the business. We moved the following spring, and it was a blissful summer.' She stopped walking and looked into Jenna's face, her own expression sliding into sadness. 'But it was a difficult winter. Will felt so cut off. By the following autumn, he said he couldn't face another winter here. I didn't want to leave. In the end, he moved to Glasgow. He's making a go of it there — he's had a few exhibitions.'

Saddened by this, Jenna pressed her

hand. 'So you keep in touch?'

'From time to time.' Rachel began walking towards the door of the hall, where a couple were entering the building. A thread of music seeped out, then disappeared when the door closed behind them. Then she turned to her companion with a bright smile. 'Well, that's my story. I expect the same from you in return.'

Jenna's heart thumped in her chest. 'Not much to say, really.' She tried to sound nonchalant. 'I was in the music business in London, in recording. I was overworked, became ill, and realised that I'd had enough. I didn't know what I was going to do instead, but when Aunt Morag broke her wrists, it was a chance for me to be useful.'

Rachel turned to her as she opened the door. The sound of accordion and fiddle burst into the night and engulfed them. 'Arasay is a wonderful place. I needed to stay here — I couldn't follow Will. Maybe you'll stay too.' Though she smiled, her eyes were sad. Jenna realised that Rachel's decision must have been difficult.

Jenna shrugged as she stepped into the warmth. 'We'll see.' Then something crossed her mind and she put out a hand to hold Rachel back. 'Have you heard if that man was identified, the one who was found dead on the road?'

A crease appeared between Rachel's eyebrows. 'That was terrible, wasn't it? No, all I've heard is that he was completely unknown. It's a bit worrying. Nothing like that has happened in the time I've lived here.'

Jenna nodded, but the tension was swept away when she was faced with the figures twirling on the dance floor, the stamping of feet, the laughter and whoops of dancers and spectators.

People called out greetings as they wove their way through the hall and found a table with some spaces. Jenna's eyes were immediately drawn to the stage where the band was in full swing. The three men were playing accordion, fiddle, and guitar. At the end of the dance, the company all broke into applause. The fiddle player bent down to retrieve a pint of beer, and took a sip. As his gaze swept the hall it rested on Rachel and he waved at her.

'Come on up, Rachel — I've got the bodhran here. We could do with a bit of rhythm.'

The object of his attention looked flustered, her cheeks stained pink. 'But I'm a novice! I've never played in public before.'

'Then it's time you did — and it's best to do it in front of friends.'

She turned to Jenna. 'Do you mind if I leave you for a short time?'

Jenna waved her on and sat back to watch the band begin another set. Rachel turned out to be very competent in adding her rhythm, laughing with enjoyment. The violinist watched her as she played — was there a spark there, Jenna wondered? Or maybe he was just checking that she was all right. Jenna eventually turned her attention to the dancers. There were quite a few children there this evening. With a start, Jenna recognised the little daughter of Jake Redman, partnering a boy with dark hair and glasses.

Jenna's feet tapped instinctively to the rhythm of the music, and her body felt ready to spring into action. Once the reel ended and Rachel returned, flushed and pleased with herself, a grey-haired man asked them to dance. Jenna hesitated. 'It's an awfully long time since I danced in a ceilidh — I probably won't know the steps.'

The man brushed away her doubts. 'It won't take you long to pick them up. It's a Dashing White Sergeant. I need you both to make a group.'

Her face lit up. 'I think I remember that one.'

She was soon laughing along with the others in the exhilaration of dancing. How wonderful it felt to have the blood coursing round her body with exertion, to grasp hands and swing round, and move her feet along with the other dancers. Some of the men were wearing kilts, which added to the ambience.

The next hour sped past in a flurry of colour, music and delight. While doing a barn dance, where they moved on to different partners regularly, Jenna partnered Rachel, taking the man's part, and at one point she found herself dancing with Jake's daughter.

'Hello!' Jenna said over the noise of the band. 'I've met your daddy at the bookshop — I'm Jenna, and I've just come to work there.'

The little girl responded with a bright smile. 'I'm Talli. These dances are such fun.'

But they only had a few moments together, and the little girl twirled round and moved on to the next partner. As Jenna danced with a selection of new partners, she found her attention wavering while her feet continued the steps. Was Jake here? Maybe he wasn't the dancing kind.

Once the music stopped, her eyes followed Talli. The girl joined an older woman with artfully coloured blonde hair, who must be her grandmother. Then Jenna's heart gave a thump as she noticed Jake. He was wearing a kilt in muted tartan, with a dark blue shirt. What was it about a fit man in a kilt that made a woman's pulses race? But her buoyancy faltered at the sight of the dark-haired woman deep in conversation with him, holding the hand of the little boy that Talli had been dancing with earlier. They all sat down together, and her mood downshifted. Every few seconds the woman would touch his arm and smile, as if they were a couple. Stupid of me, she thought ruefully. Of course he would have someone special on the island.

Rachel's appearance beside her brought her out of her reverie. 'It's the break now. Coming for a drink? I'll introduce you to the band if you like.'

Brightening at the prospect, Jenna followed her into the kitchen, where people were queuing for tea and soft drinks.

6

The guitarist looked up with a welcoming beam when Rachel approached.

'Grand job, Rachel! You're getting really good. Will you play again after the break?'

Flushed, Rachel agreed, then introduced Jenna. 'She's Morag's great niece, come to give her a hand at home and in the bookshop.'

The guitarist held out his hand. 'Good for you! How is Morag? I'm Ruaridh, by the way.'

As Jenna took his hand she found his cheerful manner charming. He was probably around thirty, with short, fair hair. She realised this must be the man who operated the delivery service. 'Morag's improving each day, though she's still rather tired. Thanks for delivering the books by the way. We were open this afternoon and sold quite a few.'

'Glad to hear it. I'm not much of a reader, myself — I'm more of a music man.'

'Ruaridh has a wonderful singing voice,' Rachel added. 'He's a real hit with the visitors. Are you singing tonight?' she asked him.

He took a swig from his bottle of beer before replying with a grin, 'Aye, after the break, before we get into the next sets.'

'Better get out your earplugs, then,' the accordion player commented with a grin. 'Ruaridh could stand in for a foghorn when he gets going.' His brown hair was greying at the temples, and he had a weatherbeaten face.

'Don't listen to Craig!' Rachel was indignant. 'You'll hear for yourself.'

The fiddle player, Hamish, was also introduced. He appeared to be around Jenna's age. She noticed again that he gravitated to Rachel as they all chatted for a while. It came out that Craig was a farmer, and Hamish was his cousin. He worked on the

75

Arasay estate as a gardener.

'So what did you do before coming to Arasay?' Craig asked.

Jenna's heart sank. Why did everyone always want to know her past? She trotted out the same story, about working in the music business. She let them think that she was in admin.

'And do you play an instrument yourself?' he followed up. Of course, the band members would be interested in another musician. She swallowed, and answered, 'Yes — flute and piano.'

Ruaridh was interested as well, now. 'Are you any good? A flute would sound great in the band.'

Taken aback, Jenna could only stammer, 'Well, I studied both at university for a couple of years.'

'Oh, a classical nut!' Craig's tone was teasing.

'No, I like all kinds of music.' She pulled herself up short before she could blurt out any more. That was the trouble, when she was with musicians — she wanted to share. To stop herself revealing her secret, she took a drink.

Craig warned them that the break was nearly over, so the two women left the band to prepare for the second half.

'Time to exercise your ears,' Craig said through the microphone. 'Now everyone, please welcome our very own Ruaridh MacAllister, the corncrake of Arasay.'

This elicited a burst of mirth from the audience, as the corncrake was a bird renowned for its loud scratchy call. The noise soon died down as Ruaridh came to stand at the front of the stage. He looked the epitome of a Scottish bard with his kilt and his *Braveheart* style shirt, open at the neck and laced down the front. Craig played an introduction, and Ruaridh began to sing.

Jenna felt the hair on the back of her neck stand up as the pure tenor voice poured into the hall, singing the famous Burns song, *My Love is Like a Red, Red Rose*. Jenna was familiar with the song, but it was astonishing to hear it performed live, and with such touching sincerity. His wasn't an obviously trained voice, but it was naturally good and he clearly practised regularly. By the end of the song, she was blinking away tears. When the closing notes died away, there was a brief silence of appreciation before the applause erupted around them.

Jenna joined in, turning to Rachel. 'What a surprise! I can't believe how beautifully he sang.'

Rachel's eyes were sparkling. 'It caught me the same way, the first time I heard him. Apparently he started singing solos in church as a boy, so everyone on the island knows about his talent. Naturally, the visitors love him. That's why he's cultivated these classic Scottish songs.'

Grinning at his reception, Ruaridh sat back in his place and picked up his guitar. Craig spoke into the micro-phone. 'Now, ladies and gents — take your partners for the *Gay Gordons*.' There was a shuffling of feet and scraping of chairs.

Suddenly Jenna felt a firm hand on her shoulder. 'May I trouble you to partner me for this dance, Jenna?' The deep voice came from behind her.

Even before she had whirled round, she knew who it was. When she looked into Jake's warm, smiling eyes, her heart leapt. 'I'm not sure if I can remember all the steps . . . '

Jake grasped her hand, pulling her to her feet, and the strength in his arm filled her with energy. 'No worries — I'll guide you round. Once you've completed a couple of rounds, you'll be fine.'

Jenna looked over to where his family and friends had been sitting, and was surprised to see that it was empty. 'Where are your family?'

'My mother has taken Talli home to bed. They're getting a lift from another friend who's taking her son home. I thought I'd stay a bit longer. I never got the chance to dance with you earlier.'

Jenna stifled a gasp. Had he stayed

just for her? Before she had time to think, the music began, and soon she was lost in the steps. The blood coursed round her body as she skipped and twirled. He asked her for a second dance, which was *Strip The Willow*. Each time Jake swung her round, his kilt swirling and his strong arm grasping hers, she felt a thrill. Then he would send her to the next man down the line while he swung the next woman, and they would come back to the centre, their eyes locked all the time they were touching. By the end her whole body was tingling.

Jake glanced at the clock on the wall. 'I shall have to go, I'm afraid. My mother will want to get on home.' He pressed her hands. 'I hope you've enjoyed our Arasay revelry.'

Her cheeks glowed. 'It was wonderful!'

Before he turned away, he said, 'I hope you'll come to the next ceilidh.'

'I'll do my best.'

Then he was gone, and she went

back to her seat, feeling the lustre had gone from her evening.

Next morning one of Morag's friends called to walk with her to church. 'It'll be good to stretch my legs,' her aunt said as she left the house. 'Are you sure you don't want to come?'

'Maybe another time,' Jenna replied. She didn't feel like being paraded before everyone again. It was quite a strain having to make up a past that wasn't her own. 'I think I'll go for a walk. I'll be back in time to make the Sunday dinner, so you don't need to worry.'

Although the sun was shining, Jenna didn't trust it to stay dry, as there were clouds on the misty hills of the next island on the horizon. She dressed in her winter walking trousers and hiking boots. Once she had zipped up her padded waterproof jacket, she slung a pair of binoculars round her neck, borrowed from the hall stand. She didn't want to miss any wildlife.

She set off down the road towards

the port in a brisk wind. The ferry wouldn't arrive until five o'clock, so the road was quiet. A few dog walkers passed her before she passed through the deserted port and took the route north.

After about a mile, a path broke off to lead down to a small beach. Unable to resist, Jenna clambered down over the rocks, and began walking along the sand. From time to time she would lift the binoculars to survey the shoreline. There were birds poking around in the shallows looking for food, and she recognised black and white oyster catchers with their pointed orange beaks, mingling with the seagulls. The sea was choppy, and she surveyed the wave, wondering if the shadows she was seeing were the shapes of seals or dolphins. But despite her concentration, the water held no prizes for her today.

She headed inland again, back to the road. Jenna had consulted the map before she left, and knew where she was planning to go. It was a relief to find that the tracks were easy to find.

She paused for a moment to let a car go past before she continued along the road. The elderly male driver gave her a pleasant wave, so she responded in like manner. A warm glow was spreading inside her. It was good to be accepted for who she was here, not as a music star, but just as Morag's great niece. She'd been out walking with her father in Northumberland, so was no stranger to the outdoors, but somehow here she felt safe, embraced by nature and by the islanders. Her mind was still fizzing with the music at the ceilidh. She must get out her flute later and play some tunes, she decided.

Once she reached the road she soon spotted the signpost she had recognised yesterday when out with Isobel. Ballintroon, her grandparents' former house. A flicker of excitement grew in her as she set off down the bumpy track, set into two grooves from motor vehicles passing up and down. How much had it changed?

The road curved down and round a rocky outcrop, and there it forked — one path leading down to the sea, no doubt to another beach, the other with an open gate. This one led to her grandparents' former home, a place she hadn't seen since she was ten years old. Jenna hesitated for a moment, wondering if the new owners would mind if she walked up to the house. Well, at least she could have a look at it from here. She scrambled up a mossy bank, overgrown with old thistles, and lifted the binoculars up to gaze through them.

Excitement caught her at the magnified building which appeared in her lenses. Yes, it was just as she remembered. The door was painted green now, not black as it had been in her childhood, but apart from that it looked just as welcoming as it had been when Granny and Grandpa lived there. So engrossed was she, that she didn't notice the approaching car until a sharp voice called out to her. 'What do you think you're doing? Don't you know that this is private property?'

7

Jenna swung round towards the owner of the voice. She found herself facing the young woman that she had seen talking to Jake at the ceilidh yesterday, confronting her through the open window of her car. Her face would have been pretty, had it not been for the frown that lowered her brows. The dark shoulder-length hair was pulled back into a practical ponytail.

Jenna took a step towards her. 'I'm sorry, I didn't mean to intrude.' In the back of the car she could see two children, the little boy who had been at the dance, and she also recognised Talli.

'We don't like strangers snooping. There are plenty of places for tourists to go on the island, without intruding on our personal lives.'

Jenna was shocked at how vehement the woman was, after the friendliness of everyone else she had met since coming to Arasay. 'I'm not a tourist. I'm Morag Buchanan's great niece, and I've come to help her out in the bookshop.'

'What's going on?' A male voice called out.

To her surprise, Jake was approaching swiftly with long strides.

'Why, Jenna! What are you doing here? Out for a walk?' To her relief he was smiling. She couldn't have borne it if he was also unfriendly.

'I'm sorry, I wasn't snooping. It's just that my grandfather once owned this house, and I used to visit it when I was a child. I just wanted to see how much I remembered.'

He smiled. 'Of course, it was Malcolm McCrinan's home.' He turned to the woman in the car, who was still frowning. 'It's all right, Kezia. Talli can get out here and we can walk home together. Thanks for taking her to church.'

At his words, Talli jumped out of the back of the car, shouting, 'Thanks, Auntie Kezia,' and ran up to Jake. She gave Jenna a smile before throwing herself at her father, who hugged her tightly.

Kezia's brows were still lowered while she set off back down the lane. Jenna realised that the reason she hadn't heard the car was that it was electric, and the wind had disguised its approach.

'Your friend was angry with me — I'm sorry. I didn't realise it would be a problem.'

'She's very protective, but you don't need to worry. Would you like to come in for a coffee?'

Wondering what Kezia would think about this offer, Jenna glanced briefly down the road at the retreating car. With a sense of defiance, she turned to Jake, and couldn't help smiling as she replied, 'Yes, please! As long as it's no trouble.'

He ushered her through the gate. Talli danced off towards the house on wiry legs, her blue skirt blowing in the wind.

Jenna laughed. 'She's a poppet. I danced briefly with her at the ceilidh.'

With parental pride, Jake grinned back. 'You don't have to tell me that — but she does have her moments. She can be very stubborn when it's time for bed.'

'Talli is an unusual name — is it short for something?'

'Tallulah — that's her American heritage. Her mother was from the US. She died a few years back.' A shadow seemed to cross his face.

'I'm so sorry,' Jenna murmured, wondering if he was still feeling raw about it. They had reached the door, and she studied the façade of the building. 'It's just the way I remember it.' The house had two main storeys, with two dormer windows on the attic floor. She pointed to the right hand window, which faced the sea. 'I had that bedroom up in the eaves when we stayed here. My brother had the other one.'

Jake beckoned her indoors, following

Talli. The little girl stood at the foot of the stairs. 'Come up and see my room. It's the best one!' Small feet pounding on the treads, she ran up the stairs then paused to see if anyone would follow.

At Jake's nod of agreement, Jenna began to ascend. On the upper floor they walked along the landing to the end room. It was decorated with pale pink walls, liberally hung with posters of birds and animals, and a large photo portrait of Jake with Talli on a beach. There was a collection of stuffed toys on a shelf. Talli reached for the end toy, a beautiful brown teddy bear. 'Look, this is what Daddy brought me from his last trip. I've called him Brian.'

Jenna stroked the plush head. 'Brian Bear — he's lovely.'

'Daddy always brings me a cuddly animal like the ones he's been filming. Though, of course, real wild animals aren't cuddly!'

'No.' Jenna grinned. 'My parents used to sleep in this room when we came for holidays. I used to sleep in the top of the house.'

'Which one?' Talli took her hand and dragged her to the steep steps that led up to the attics. Once they had climbed up, Jenna pointed to the little room she had slept in as a child. 'That's Daddy's workroom,' Talli explained. 'He might not let us go in.'

'Yes, you can.' Jake's deep voice echoed in the tiny landing as he followed them up. He reached past them and opened the door. Jenna could see a large desk with a computer, and deep open shelves strewn with camera equipment. A tall tripod leaned against the wall by the window.

Jenna stepped inside the room. 'The wallpaper's still the same.' With one finger she traced the old-fashioned flowers on the wall.

'I just didn't have time to redecorate it before I wanted to use it for work.'

Jenna gazed for a long time out of the window, remembering the times she had crept from her bed, and had stared at the sea in the long, light May evenings. She sighed with contentment.

After Talli had given her a quick peep into the other bedrooms, the child took her hand and led her downstairs.

Jake made them coffee and poured a juice for Talli, then they took their mugs through to the living room. It was airy and open, with a long window looking back towards the road. Talli was kneeling on one of two large settees, walking a small toy dog along the windowsill. She jumped down and joined Jake in one of the armchairs. Jenna perched opposite them on the settee.

They chatted about the island and how it had been when Jenna used to visit. After a while, she looked out at the sweeping island panorama, thinking how perfect it was in comparison to the view from her flat in London. She was about to say just that when she caught herself. No, the less she said about her past, the better. Looking round at the paraphernalia of family life, the child's paintings on the wall, the coffee table and the wood-burning stove with a basket full of logs, she felt as if she had stepped from a wild nightmare into real life.

Talli soon bored of the adult talk, and jumped down to play with her toy dog on the other settee.

Jake followed her fondly with his eyes. 'Talli wants us to get a dog, but it's just not feasible as I'm away so much, and the burden would fall on my mother. She lives in the cottage down the road, but she moves in here when I'm away.'

Disappointed that he might leave soon, Jenna asked, 'When are you going away?'

'Thankfully my next project isn't too far away, filming wildlife in the Cairngorm mountain range. In the meantime, while I'm at home I'll be working on some photography.'

'That sounds interesting. I hope to see some wildlife on my walks. I'm building up my stamina, as I had a bout of pneumonia a year ago.'

'Well, you can't get anywhere wilder than a Scottish island. The fresh air will do you good.'

Before leaving, she turned to him, as a thought crossed her mind. 'Jake, I've noticed some flickering lights at night a couple of times, over in the direction of the sea when looking from my bedroom. I can't see any houses over that way, and wondered if you knew what it could be?'

His brow furrowed. 'No, that sounds rather odd. Could you maybe show me some time?'

Startled at this offer, Jenna stuttered, 'Of course, thanks.' She stood up. 'It was really kind of you to show me round Ballintroon. It's brought back many happy memories. Bye, Talli.'

Jake walked with her to the door, the little girl following to stand by his side so they could wave her off. 'Come again — you're always welcome.'

Jenna's heart lifted as she returned their farewell, zipping up her coat on her way towards the gate. As she turned

94

back towards the path, her eye caught a bright flash in the heather beyond, and she stopped for a moment. Was somebody watching them through binoculars?

Then she dismissed it as a fancy. She had to stop thinking like a celebrity. No doubt it was a birdwatcher. A few visitors were already trickling on to the island. The following week they would be opening the bookshop every afternoon, back to its summer hours. She pushed the intriguing 'Jared' and his daughter from her mind and set off back towards Balloch with long strides.

8

As the days went by, Jenna found that she was waking with a smile on her face, looking forward to what was ahead of her. The bookshop was a delight, and she was beginning to feel at home in the surroundings. Morag left her on her own on the Wednesday, and after an initial flutter of anxiety, she soon found that she was happy dealing with any customers.

About half an hour before closing, Isobel entered, shaking raindrops from her hair. She paused to hold the door as a man in his forties came up behind her, wearing a fleece jacket with a hood. He ignored Isabel's smile and stalked straight up to the counter, trailing some mud in on his boots, Jenna noticed. Another job for later.

But she greeted him pleasantly, as he was a customer. 'Good afternoon. How may I help you?' She tried to ignore the unease that surfaced as his large presence shadowed her from the light.

'I need a local map. Something with all the little roads and islands on it.' His voice was gruff and had a distinctly transatlantic accent.

'Certainly. What sort of activity is it for?'

'That's my business, lady. Just get me a map.'

Jenna's eyes flickered to Isobel, registering their neighbour's barely audible intake of breath at the brusque remark. 'Of course. These are the most detailed. There are two scales of map here. This one is a larger scale. Then we have the free tourist maps that show clearly the new marked hiking routes.'

Thank goodness for Isobel's presence. This was the first customer that she hadn't liked at all. Everyone else had been friendly.

He tossed one of the maps back on to the counter. 'I've got this one.' After a minute looking at the larger scale map, he nodded. 'Okay, this will do. And I'll take a free map as well.' He handed over a credit card, which Jenna processed. She slipped the maps into a paper bag and handed back the card and receipt. With a grunt, he took the bag and unzipped a pocket on the inside of his fleece, where he stowed it. As he turned to leave, the credit card slipped to the floor unnoticed.

Isobel had spotted it, and picked it up to pass to him. 'You've dropped your card!'

As he snatched it from her hand with a glare, the schoolteacher recoiled. Without a word he stomped over to the exit and left the shop, leaving the door to slam shut in his wake.

'Phew! He was grouchy!' Isobel commented.

'Thank goodness he's left — and I hope he doesn't come back.' Relaxing now, Jenna asked, 'What can I do for you today?'

'I have a special order that should have come in last week. Is it here yet?'

Jenna scrolled through the orders on the computer. 'Yes, it's arrived. Twenty copies of *A First Scottish Recorder Book*.' Nipping to the back room, she brought the box back in and humped it on to the desk. 'All paid for, I see.'

'Yes, it's for the school. I'm trying to expand the music, as we haven't had any instrumental tuition for a couple of years. I thought it would be good if they all learned an instrument from the age of seven.'

Jenna flicked through the book. 'This looks like fun. It has nice colour illustrations, too.'

'I've heard you playing the flute at nights.'

'Sorry, I didn't mean to disturb anyone.'

'No, I'm not complaining — quite the opposite. You sound very good.' Isobel gave her a penetrating look. 'What I'm trying to say is — would you consider doing the recorder instruction? We have a budget for visiting tutors. It would be in groups of two, just fifteen minutes per pair.' As Jenna opened her mouth to protest, she quickly went on, 'They're nice children. I can't promise prodigies, but they're well-behaved and interested in all sorts of things. Please think about it.'

'I really don't know, Isobel. I've never done any teaching.' Jenna's mind was whirling at this idea.

'You don't have to give me an answer today. It's the end of term on Friday, and it wouldn't start until after the holiday. You could come in one morning a week. By then, Morag will be recovering and I'm sure she'll be in the shop every day, so you won't have so much to do.'

After a pause, Jenna nodded. 'All right, I'll think about it. But I can't make any promises.'

'I understand. Thanks, Jenna. I'll be away now and let you get on.'

Next morning Jenna walked with Morag along to the health centre. 'We have two doctors, and of one of them is Ian Drummond, Caitlin's husband,' her great aunt said. 'I wonder if he's gone to the mainland yet for the baby's arrival?'

Morag was soon ushered in to see Dr Drummond, who cut off her cast. Jenna liked his boyish demeanour, and his cheerful excitement that he was to be on the afternoon ferry to be with his wife for the birth of their baby.

'Gosh, my arm looks so thin.' Morag gazed in dismay at the pale limb that had been exposed.

'Your muscles haven't been used for a few weeks. Don't worry, they'll restore in time, especially after you soak the arm as I described. Pick up a leaflet at reception with exercises to do. Just begin gently. Any problems, don't hesitate to come back. We're always here to help.'

'Thanks doctor. Give my love to Caitlin, and let us know about the baby as soon as you can.'

'Thanks, I will. Take care, now.'

As they left his room, an older doctor was waiting at the door, and gave

Morag a brief greeting before calling out to Ian, 'I have a callout — will you have time to deal with my last two patients as well as yours before you go?'

A frown appeared on Ian's brow. 'Yes, I can, but I hope there are no complications.'

'No, they're routine follow-ups I believe. But I must attend this. It's Craig McPherson — a suspected dislocated shoulder.'

The two women gasped at this. 'Not Craig from the band?' Jenna exclaimed.

Dr Lewis turned to her. 'Yes, he was dealing with a cow that had wandered into a bog. Farming can be a dangerous business.'

'I do hope he'll be all right,' Morag said.

'Indeed,' Ian agreed, and went to call his next patient. Later that day, having soaked and rubbed moisturising cream into Morag's arm, Jenna wondered about Craig's injury. 'That'll be a blow for the band. He can't possibly play his accordion, can he?'

'I doubt it. They'll have to manage with just Ruaridh on guitar for the first of the music sessions at the hotel this Friday. But we'll be getting an influx of tourists on Saturday, when the school holidays begin, and there's a ceilidh planned. They'll have to use recorded music.'

Jenna nodded, but mused that it was a pity as the live music was so rousing. She thought nothing more of it until the next morning, when Ruaridh knocked at the back door of the bookshop, a large box in his arms.

He placed it on the workbench. 'Here's your delivery. There's another box in the van. Let's hope you get lots of customers over the next two weeks, to kick start the new season.'

'Thanks, Ruaridh.' She signed the delivery note, then added, 'How's Craig? We heard about his accident at the surgery.'

The smile slipped from his face. 'Not good. He's going to be out of action for a few weeks.'

'I'm so sorry! How will he manage with the farm?'

Ruaridh tucked the delivery note into a folder. 'Luckily he farms with his older brother, Duncan. He was out with Craig when it happened. Cattle have the unfortunate tendency to wander into bogs, and though they try to prevent it, this one slipped through. He's a good bull, and they didn't want to lose him.'

'Of course not.' Jenna was well aware that valuable stock needed to be protected. 'Did they manage to rescue the bull?'

Ruaridh gave a wry grin. 'Oh, aye, the beast's fine. But Craig's not pleased about being unable to play.' Then he gave her a sideways look. 'Rachel mentioned that you play the piano. I don't suppose you'd consider trying out with us? It would mean that we wouldn't lose our fee for the ceilidh. I can manage with the guitar on Friday for the session at the hotel.'

Jenna gasped. She hadn't been

expecting this. 'I don't know. I've never played ceilidh music before. I recognised a few of the melodies the other night, but I certainly couldn't perform in public without music.' She had played her own songs from memory, but it was different when you had actually written the music yourself.

His face brightened with hope. 'We'd look out a music book from somewhere. Lots of people on the island have played instruments, though of course there's a great tradition of learning by ear here. Leave it with me — I'll get back to you later.'

Panic began to rise. 'I didn't say I would — I'm probably rubbish.'

He gave her a kindly smile as he opened the door. 'Let's wait and see, shall we? You'd be doing us a huge favour. I'll be getting on now, but I'll let you know when I've sorted something out. We can rehearse tomorrow morning.'

Jenna found that her legs would hold her up no longer, and she sank into one

105

of the workroom chairs. Had people been talking about her? Could someone have joined the dots and realised who she was? Later when she returned to the house, she poured out all her anxiety to Morag.

'I'm trying to keep a low profile here, and somehow I'm being pushed into the spotlight. The band will lose their fee if I don't help them out. But I'm scared. I like being just Jenna. Linnet is in the past, and not who I am any more.' She chopped a carrot furiously while she spoke.

Morag, sitting with her hand against her shoulder to help with its rehabilitation, shook her head. 'I think you're magnifying this out of proportion. There's no reason why anyone should associate you with a former pop artist. Why not have a go? You could really enjoy it, and I know they're nice lads.'

Jenna chewed her lip as she threw the carrots into the pot and reached for a cauliflower. Maybe Ruaridh wouldn't be able to find a music book, and she would escape. But deep down, she knew that she should help them out — and she was tempted by the thought of playing music again.

When Ruaridh rang later to say Hamish had found a book with chord symbols, she took a deep breath and closed her eyes, pushing her fears away. 'All right — I'll try.'

'Great!' She could hear the smile in his voice. 'Don't worry, we'll be gentle with you. We really appreciate it, thanks.'

As she entered the village hall the next morning for the band's practice session, her legs were stiff and her eyes heavy after a restless night. What was she doing? But part of her hummed with anticipation at the thought of joining in a music group again.

Hamish was tuning his fiddle when she reached the two men. Ruaridh swung round and grinned at her. 'We brought out the digital piano. I hope it's OK.' A battered music book was sitting on the top.

After a brief warm up at the piano to loosen her fingers, she turned to look at Ruaridh and was met with a smile.

'I knew you had it in you!' he crowed. 'I could sense it.'

Jenna shook her head. 'Wait until we've rehearsed before you make any judgement. Are we ready to start?'

'Why don't we start with a *Dashing White Sergeant*? We'll start with a chord, and if you could join in playing the melody and just put in some simple chords to flesh it out?' He picked up his guitar and looked at her encouragingly.

A couple of hours sped by as they went through the dances they would need for the ceilidh. By the end of the rehearsal, Jenna was tired, but satisfied that she had coped all right, and she felt as if her whole consciousness had expanded with the joy of playing music in a band again. Not that she wanted to go back to Urban Hawk, but she was aware that she needed music in her life.

Walking back to Morag's house, she hummed their last tune to herself. But as she reached home her stomach gave a sudden lurch. What if one of the visitors was to recognise her?

9

The next evening, dressed in a black shirt and trousers, with Morag's tartan sash draped from her shoulder, Jenna prepared to leave for the ceilidh.

'Do you think I look OK? Do I look different enough not to be recognised?'

Morag reached out and patted her arm. 'Jenna, dear, you would be surprised at how you've changed. It's not just that Linnet's scarlet hair has been replaced by a golden crop, but instead of the harrowed, thin face with heavy eye makeup and dark lips, I see fresh, glowing skin, and a ready smile. That makes you a totally different person. I doubt if your own band members would recognise you now.'

Jenna's shallow breathing began to deepen as Morag's words penetrated. After a moment, she said, 'I suppose

I'm lucky I don't have any distinguishing features — no aquiline nose, or luscious full lips. I'm just a regular-looking girl.'

Morag gave a chuckle. 'And a very pretty girl too, Jenna. It's time you realised that you're an attractive young woman.'

Once the ceilidh dancers were beginning to arrive, doubts began to assail Jenna once more. She wished she could just run out of the door. After all, many of the people were islanders who were used to Craig's experience and deft artistry on his accordion. But soon the doors had shut and Ruaridh was starting things off.

'To those of you who are visitors, I'd like to tell you that we have a new band member tonight. Jenna has kindly stepped in at short notice because our regular accordion player, Craig, has had an accident and is unfortunately out of action for a week or two. I know you'll all be behind her as she's never played for a ceilidh before, but I can assure

111

you that she's a very capable musician. Jenna, everyone!'

The applause and whistles broke out, at which Jenna stood up uncertainly, her cheeks flaming, to acknowledge their support. Then they played the first chord and began the *Dashing White Sergeant*. Her hands trembled at first, but as in the rehearsal she became immersed in the music and her nerves dissolved, instead feeling the euphoria of playing and sharing the music.

At the break time, one or two islanders came over and greeted her. 'She's doing great, isn't she?' Ruaridh added as he put away his guitar. Then one of the tourists came up with her phone and took a selfie of herself with the band.

Jenna felt as if her heart was going to explode out of her chest. Resisting the urge to grab the woman's phone and delete the photo, she pushed her way through the crowds to the exit. The air was cool, and she stood for a few minutes, shivering and holding her arms round herself. Dread engulfed her that the selfie woman could put the picture on her social media, and Jenna would be recognised.

'Hi, are you OK?'

Whirling round, she realised that Jake Redman was standing behind her in the doorway, holding two bottles of beer. For a moment she felt disoriented from her surroundings, but then blinked a few times and took a deep breath. 'I . . . just needed a moment. I felt a bit overwhelmed.'

Jake stepped outside to stand beside her, and held out one of the bottles he was carrying. 'Would you like a beer?'

Jenna nodded. 'Thanks.' She took a mouthful of the cool drink, allowing the bubbles to froth on her tongue before swallowing. Finding its coolness calmed her, she drank some more, then looked up at him.

His expression was warm. 'I came along this evening to see if you'd like another dance, and here you are, playing in the band. You never mentioned that you were a talented piano player.'

She turned her head away, trying to shield herself from his scrutiny. She knew instinctively that Jake wouldn't betray her real identity, but people always treated her differently when they discovered that she was famous. The emotions that engulfed her whenever she was in his company were exciting and new. Disclosing her past would only spoil whatever might develop.

'Did it sound all right?' she managed to say.

'Fantastic! I would never have known that you'd only had one rehearsal yesterday if Ruaridh hadn't told me. You've saved the band, and done the island proud this evening.'

Tears pricked her eyes at his sincerity. But what surprised her more was when he reached out a hand to touch her chin and turn her face towards him. Concern was etched on his face as he gazed deep into her eyes.

'What is it, Jenna? What's upsetting you?'

She gave a brittle laugh. 'It's nothing. I guess I'm a bit tired.'

He lowered his arm to his side again, but his gaze never left her face. 'You'll have a busy week ahead of you, with the shop being open for the Easter visitors. But how would you like to come round the gardens of Arasay House with me on one morning? They're beginning to show spring flowers, and it's very attractive.'

Surprise jolted her out of her worries. 'That's the Laird's house, isn't it? I've heard that the gardens are worth a visit. Are you sure you have the time, with Talli being on holiday from school?'

He laughed. 'That wee girl has a better social life than I do. She'll be playing with various friends throughout the week. She's on a sleepover tonight for a friend's birthday. She'll be cranky as anything tomorrow because they won't get much sleep, I'll bet.'

Jenna couldn't help smiling as the

image of innocent childhood filled her mind. Then the door to the hall opened again. Hamish poked his head out. 'There you are, Jenna! Ruaridh's getting ready to start the second half with a song, so we're setting up again.'

She handed her empty bottle to Jake. 'Thanks for the beer — I'd better go. But I'd like to come round the gardens — which day?'

They agreed on Wednesday, and she slipped back into the hall. Back at home later in her bedroom, Jenna allowed herself to give in to the curiosity that had been rolling around at the back of her mind. She booted up her laptop and began searching for Linnet and Urban Hawk. It was something she had resisted doing for a long time, as she didn't want to read all the speculation.

It only took a few seconds for the results to come up on the screen. Her breath became short as she read the headlines. 'Urban Hawk's Linnet goes underground!' read one. Others also screamed sensational headlines. 'Devon sues unresponsive Linnet for rights to Hawk songs.' 'Urban Hawk in trouble after Linnet cancels tours.' 'Devon's devastation at his partner's treachery — can Hawk survive?'

But as she scanned each article, her panic turned to anger. How dare he make out she had abandoned them! Their agent had issued a press statement when she had pulled out of the tour due to illness. She had also sent Devon formal word via her solicitor that she wanted out of the band. He'd tried to persuade her to change her mind, but she was adamant she didn't want to continue. She had left them the use of her songs, just glad to get some income from record sales.

Finally, closing the laptop screen with a snap, she sat fuming. She needed to chivvy her solicitor. It was time to fight back! She rang Richard on the Monday. While speaking with him she kept her gaze on the wild landscape leading towards the sea. Today it was grey and stormy, as if it had chosen to match her own turbulent feelings.

'Don't worry, Linnet, everything's under control,' he soothed. Jenna swallowed her irritation at the use of her stage name, but before she could snap at him, the thought entered her head that it was best if he used it always when making statements, so he ought not to get used to calling her Jenna. 'Do we have a date for the hearing?' she finally queried.

'Yes, we do — there's a preliminary in June. You won't need to be there, as it's really just to set a date for the main trial later in the year.'

She let out her breath in relief that she wouldn't need to appear in public yet. 'Should I come to London to go through everything with you?'

'No, I could get Kieron to come up to Scotland to see you. Bright young lawyer. He's so sharp that I'll need to look out for my job.'

At last! It was time she talked it through with someone who could advise her. 'Yes, tell Kieron to come. I want to know everything to date.'

They agreed that Jenna would meet him in Glasgow two weeks after Easter. This calmed her, and by the time Jake arrived on the Wednesday, she was able to focus on him without distractions. She greeted him at the door, wearing her padded jacket, walking trousers and hiking boots.

He responded cheerfully to her. 'Glad to see you're dressed appropriately. The gardens are wild, especially after the winter. Arasay House has lots of rare exotic trees, as it's sheltered here in the lee of the other islands, and warmed by the Gulf Stream.'

It didn't take him long to drive to the gates of the estate. As they approached the sign, Jenna exclaimed in disappointment. 'Oh, it's closed.'

He grinned, and drove straight past the house. 'No need to worry. I have friends in high places.'

When they pulled into the tiny car park, he took a digital SLR camera from the back seat and slung it round his neck. Jenna assumed that his career as a well-known local photographer gave him access to the gardens. She followed him past a small tearoom which was dark and uninhabited. There was a metal barred gate to one side, and he produced a key for the padlock and opened it, ushering her through. He looped the chain back through the bars and snapped the padlock shut.

They walked down a short wooded path before it opened out to reveal an extensive lawn leading up to the whitewashed house. Jenna lost count of the windows along the side of the building, but reckoned there must be more than twenty on each of the two floors, with attic windows in the dark slate roof. By stately home standards it was modest, but its design was clean and pleasing to the eye, and impressive for a small island like Arasay. There was a footpath right round the house, but Jake told her that the only public area was the extensive wild garden. He led her down winding, criss-crossing paths, over little bridges and streams, pointing out unusual trees and bushes. They also visited a walled garden, dotted with late crocuses and nodding daffodils.

Every now and then he would take a photo, sometimes spending a while focusing the shot, other times snapping spontaneously.

'I wish I'd brought my camera,' Jenna said as she watched him photographing the light through the trees. 'I bought a DSLR last year, and although I'm not an expert, I've been pleased with the pictures I've captured.'

He turned to her with a grin. 'Next time you must bring it with you, and I'll give you some tips.'

It was good to think that there would be a next time, she thought as they left the walled garden and headed towards some tall trees. Before they reached the trees, he took her hand, his touch making her jump, but he put his finger to his lips and slowed her down. 'There's something magical ahead,' he whispered. 'Follow me.'

Still holding her hand, he moved slowly through the trees, which thinned out to reveal a large pond. Jenna gasped at the beauty of the trees reflected in the still water, cut with ripples from ducks crossing its surface. A pair of mute swans were dipping their beaks in the water over by the reeds. Jake and Jenna crept to the edge of the water, in the cover of some bushes. Some bird feeders had been hung on the trees at either side of the clearing, and small birds were flitting out of the trees to peck at the nuts. Jenna recognised chaffinches, blue tits and greenfinches. Jake lifted his camera to capture shots of them feeding.

Although Jenna was entranced by the wildlife at close quarters, she found her eyes constantly straying to Jake, loving watching him at work. The intensity on his face, the concentration and dedication stirred something inside her. For several minutes he was lost in his work, then finally looked at her. 'Enough?' he mouthed.

She nodded, and they crept away from the edge again. Once they had distanced themselves from the pond and were walking back through the paths, Jake began speaking in a normal voice. 'Too many visitors barge past the pond, talking loudly, and they miss the magic of the inhabitants. I'd like to see the path routed further back, with maybe some sort of deflecting barrier so that the sound of voices doesn't disturb the birds.'

'I'm sure the owners would respect your judgement, if you pushed for it.'

He grunted and looked at his watch. 'It's coming up to midday. You'll need to be getting back in time to open up the bookshop.'

'I can't believe how quickly the time has gone.'

'So you enjoyed it? Would you like to see some coastal wildlife some time? We might even spot some otters if we're lucky. Maybe next week?'

Jenna slowed her pace, frowning. 'I'd love to, but I have to go to Glasgow, which means I'll be off the island for a couple of days.'

'Hello, Jake! I heard you were in the garden.'

Both of them swung round at the sound of a man's voice. The grey-haired newcomer was probably around sixty years old, dressed in a tweed jacket and brown corduroy trousers. Jenna realised that they were only a few metres from the garden entrance once more.

Jake greeted the man. 'Hello David. Good to see you — how are you? How are all the family?'

David smiled and shook Jake's hand. 'Well, thanks. Portia's flown to Edinburgh for a shopping trip, and has taken Daisy with her. It's a bit of a treat for her, as she's about to sit her A Levels, and we want to keep her calm.'

They exchanged scraps of news about their families, then Jake turned back to Jenna and introduced her. 'Jenna, this is my uncle David, my mother's younger brother. David, meet

Jenna Davidson. She's Morag Buchanan's great niece, and is here to help out as Morag unfortunately damaged her wrists in a fall.'

'Pleased to meet you — I'm so sorry to hear about Morag. Are you Shona's daughter?'

Surprised at his knowledge of the residents of the island, Jenna answered with an affirmative.

The older man continued, 'When I heard Jake was in the garden with a young lady, I assumed it was Kezia. So how is she doing?'

A small frown graced Jake's brow as he replied, 'She's away with Lachlan for the holiday.'

David gave a nod and changed the subject. 'I heard the police have received an identification for the body you found on your first night back. His name was Shane Green, and bizarrely it turns out that he's from California, would you believe? He's on international police books because of drug smuggling or something like that. It's a worrying situation — why would he be on Arasay, our little island out in the middle of nowhere?'

Jenna was watching Jake, and it looked as if he'd been punched in the stomach. 'California, did you say? Did they tell you the cause of death?'

'They think he tripped in the dark, hit his head and drowned in the ditch, no foul play. But I still think that there's something fishy going on, and I'm not talking about cod or haddock.' The grimness of his expression denied the levity of his words. Then he looked at Jenna and apologised. 'I shouldn't be worrying you when you've just come to the island.'

'No, don't worry. I'll be on my guard.'

David said his farewells and turned towards the house. Once he was out of earshot, Jenna said, 'I take it your uncle lives here at Arasay House.'

Jake was still looking distant, but pulled his attention back to her. 'What? Oh yes, David and his family are living in the house full-time. My grandfather doesn't live here any more, as he's ninety now and has a heart condition. He prefers to be in Edinburgh near his doctors.'

'By your grandfather, you mean the Laird? I never realised you were practically nobility.'

Jake gave a laugh, his attention fully on her now. 'They're just landowners. You probably have more McCrinan blood than I do. I just belong to a regular family. My father's a scientist, a marine biologist, but my parents divorced when I was a teenager. I occasionally bump into Dad when we're working on the same continent. Mum was a botanist with the Forestry Commission but now works for the Arasay estate, which was great for me when I brought Talli back to live here.'

Jenna followed him back towards the car. 'Jake — I hope you don't mind me asking, but you looked worried when your uncle mentioned the identity of the dead man. Did you recognise it?'

'No, I didn't know him. But it seems too much of a coincidence that he's from California.'

'Why is that?'

'My wife came from California, and my mother-in-law Gayle still lives there. I've been in a battle with her for the past four years over custody of Talli. I'm worried that she's been sending people to watch my family, and that she could be planning to snatch her away from me.'

10

Jenna was horrified. 'Surely she has no grounds to contest your right as Talli's father.'

They climbed inside the Land Rover. 'Her argument is that I'm away so often. Plus, Talli and her mother were living with Gayle when Savannah was killed in the accident.'

He sat in the driver's seat with the car keys in his hand, making no attempt to insert them into the ignition socket. 'I'm not proud of the fact that she had left me. Savannah hated being left on her own with a young child. She told me that she would never have married me if she'd known what my job really entailed. So she went back to live with her mother. Her stepfather had died the previous year, and Gayle, her mother, was running the family business — three casinos. She'd divorced from

Savannah's father when she was small, and had remarried when she was eleven. Savannah found the lifestyle glamorous, and once she went back, her mother employed a carer for Talli which meant that Savannah was free to pursue her own interests.'

Jenna, surprised by his openness, could think of nothing to reply. In truth, she was fascinated to hear the true account of his troubled marriage.

'They had been with Gayle for a year. I would visit in between jobs, but Savannah and her mother were becoming increasingly hostile towards me. Our divorce was almost through. We were beginning to argue about access to Talli. She was only four years old, and Savannah claimed that my appearances and disappearances were unsettling, and was talking of sole custody. But before we got to court, Savannah was killed in a car accident. They never told me exactly how it happened, and I suspected that she'd maybe been under the influence of drink, or worse, and

Gayle had paid to have it hushed up. I was due to take Talli away for a few days to stay with some friends in Canada, as I was to fly home to Scotland the following week. I arrived the day after the accident. Gayle wasn't at home, and the child carer told me what had happened to Savannah. They hadn't had the decency to let me know immediately. I picked up a few extra things for Talli, and left with her as soon as I could. I knew she needed stability, and I'm afraid she'd had precious little of that since she was born. My mother agreed to look after her while I was working, and we settled into this routine. Being her father, I had the right to do that. But Gayle has never given up.'

He turned and looked at Jenna, his eyes sad. 'I've never let her see her American grandmother again. I'm just too afraid that she'll steal her away from me. When I met you I'd just come from the United States and a custody hearing, which I'm pleased to say I won. But Gayle's appealing the decision. I've told Talli none of this — we just say that Grandma can't visit because she's busy in America. We've created memory books about her mother, as advised by child grief counsellors. We talk about Savannah a lot — I tell her about our happy times. But it's not easy.'

'Of course,' Jenna murmured. 'So how did you two meet, if you don't mind me asking?'

'I was doing a photography degree in London, and we socialised with the students from the art school, where she was studying fashion.' He gave a rueful smile. 'She was so vibrant, and I was dazzled. We had what you might call a whirlwind romance, and it blossomed when I took her to Australia with me on one of my first shoots. Naively, we got married as soon as we returned to the UK and before we knew it, she was pregnant. She was far from her own home and family, and couldn't settle in mine.'

Jenna imagined how difficult it must have been for the young couple. 'I'm so sorry,' she said.

He shrugged and started the engine. 'I didn't mean to dump all this information on you. But I thought it would be better to explain the situation. I'd like to think of us becoming . . . closer.' He turned and gazed deep into her eyes.

It was like a thunderbolt beaming from his eyes into hers. Jenna felt as if something had snapped within her, whether it was her resistance, or her inhibitions, she didn't know. She had to resist the urge to wrap her arms around him and kiss away the hurt that she read in his eyes. Instead she dug her fingernails into her palms, and managed to say through dry lips, 'I'm glad you told me. I hope we'll be friends, too.'

Their eyes held for a few seconds more. It was as if the word 'friends' didn't cover what they might mean to each other. She hoped not, anyway. As she broke their gaze and turned her head briefly back to see if his uncle had gone, she knew that the situation was fraught with complications, especially as she didn't feel like baring her own soul to Jake at that moment.

When they passed through Balloch, Jenna saw Morag walking down the road arm-in-arm with Isobel. 'Look, Isobel must have decided to take her for a walk. I'm glad — it means that Morag's regaining her confidence.'

Jake raised an eyebrow. 'Good. Now, how about showing me where you saw those lights.'

'Okay.' They pulled up outside the house. Jake followed her into the hallway, and closed the door behind them before they ascended to Jenna's room. When they entered, she was conscious that it looked untidy. She'd left out a pile of clothes, and there were music books strewn on the bed. But Jake only seemed to notice the music stand.

'So what's the music for?'

'Flute — that's my main instrument. I studied it for two years at university, before I dropped out.' Seeing the question in his eyes (which she didn't want to answer), she hurried on. 'Isobel has asked me to teach recorder at the school. I'm starting next week.'

He grinned. 'Yes, the school always likes to get the children playing music. In my time, we all learned Scottish fiddle from Joan Muir. She was in her eighties then, and had been teaching violin on the island for many a year.'

'I didn't realise you were musical.'

'I wasn't bad, but I never practised because I was always out with a camera. Now, which direction were the lights?'

Jenna pointed out of the window towards the sea. Jake slipped a small pair of binoculars from his pocket and studied the landscape intently. She couldn't take her eyes from the sculpted planes of his cheeks, noticing the small lines at the side of his eyes and mouth, etched by sun and weather. His mouth was pursed in thought, and she wondered what it would feel like pressed against her own. Taking a breath, she stepped back and told herself that now was not the time to have such thoughts.

'Hmm, I can see nothing unusual. I'll take the Land Rover along and walk out to that point.'

'Don't you think you should tell the police, in case it's something illegal?' He lowered the binoculars. 'It looks as if this activity is going on at night. Once May and June come, the sky hardly goes dark for long, so there wouldn't be any cover for illegal activities.'

'Please be careful, Jake.'

He took her hand and squeezed it. 'I'm touched that you should be concerned for me, but I can assure you there's no need. I won't go too close if I think it could be dangerous.'

Jenna hardly heard his words, the sensation of physical contact sending a tingle through her fingers. Then he slid his hand behind her waist and pulled her sharply towards him. For a moment

136

they were standing almost nose to nose, then he leaned his head to one side and placed his lips firmly on her own. The gasp of surprise that opened her lips allowed him to taste her in a long exploratory kiss. Her own arms reached round his shoulders, as she revelled in the feeling of his long, muscular body against her own.

When they finally pulled apart, they said nothing, merely gazing into each other's eyes. Then the corners of his mouth twitched upwards. 'Well, where did that come from?'

A flush stained her cheeks. Then a movement outside caught her eye. 'Quick, Morag and Isobel are coming. We'd better go downstairs — she wouldn't approve of you being in my bedroom.'

When Morag entered the hall they were in the kitchen, Jake filling the kettle and Jenna taking mugs from the cupboard. They chatted for about twenty minutes before Jake took his leave, and Jenna went back upstairs.

Standing by the window where they had shared that impromptu kiss, she tried to gather her disturbed thoughts.

While she watched the Land Rover disappearing, she confessed to herself she was definitely falling for the delectable wildlife photographer. Should she encourage him, or was her life such a mess that it would be a total disaster? At least she would have some time to sort out her feelings, for he would be away for a couple of weeks from Sunday, filming in the Cairngorms mountain range. He'd promised to keep in touch.

The band was a welcome distraction. Ruaridh and Hamish asked her to play her flute with them at the session in the hotel on the Friday night. The musical camaraderie made her feel more accepted than she had done for a long time. Afterwards the three members of the band were treated to free drinks in the hotel bar, when some visitors to the island came to chat.

'Do you have any recordings we can

buy?' asked one woman. Her drawl betrayed her Australian origins.

Ruaridh apologised and replied that unfortunately they didn't. After she had left, he turned to Jenna. 'Visitors ask that more and more. It's nice to know that people like our music so much that they would take it home with them.' He grinned and took a swig from his pint.

Jenna knew that it wouldn't be difficult to arrange to record a CD with some of the band's best tunes. But now wasn't the time, especially with Craig out of action. The accordion player was sitting next to Hamish, his arm in a sling. He'd thanked Jenna for stepping in at the last minute. 'But don't let that seat get too warm,' he added. 'I'm coming back as soon as I'm able.'

Jenna assured him that she would step down as soon as he was fit. She recognised the wariness in his eyes, and that his banter hid a real warning that he didn't want anyone muscling in on his patch. That was yet another reason to keep her background secret.

The following night during the ceilidh midway break, she found a text from Jake on her phone.

'Sorry I won't see you tonight. Busy getting ready to go away, and I need to be at home to put Talli to bed. Have fun at the ceilidh. Jake x.'

Tickled by the fact that he had put 'x' at the end of the message, she sent a reply wishing him a good trip. The sound of the door opening made her swing round, thinking it might be one of the band. But it was a tall woman with dark hair, aged around thirty. It only took Jenna a few seconds to recognise her as Kezia, the mother of Lachlan, Talli's friend. Seeing the hard expression on her face, Jenna felt her defences rise.

'You're Jenna,' the newcomer said.

'That's right.'

'I just want to give you a warning. I don't know what you think you're doing, pushing yourself in here. But you're an outsider, you don't belong. Jake's spoken for. We've known each other a long time, and that's something special. Everyone knows he's mine — except you.'

Jenna had to clench her fist to stop herself gasping. 'I'm sorry, I didn't know . . .'

'Well, you do now. Leave him alone.' With these words, Kezia turned on her heel and went back into the hall, leaving Jenna feeling as if she had been slapped in the face. When she returned to the band, Ruaridh looked at her inquisitively.

'Something troubling you?'

She shook her head, her mouth tense. 'Ruaridh. I'm a bit confused. Do you know Jake Redman and Kezia, the woman over there?'

'Yes, of course — we were all at primary school together, though Jake boarded in Edinburgh later, while the rest of us went to Oban for high school.'

'Kezia just told me that she and Jake are together. Is that true?'

His eyebrows raised, Ruaridh gave a

low whistle. 'Well, that's a new one on me. Their two kids are friends, so they sometimes do things as a group. But I wasn't aware of anything more.'

Jenna felt her shoulders relaxing. It looked as if the feelings were more on Kezia's side than Jake's. Maybe he might really be free. 'Thanks.' She climbed back to take her seat at the piano.

But Ruaridh came up beside her. 'Why do you ask, Jenna — are you and Jake . . . ?'

It suddenly occurred to her that he might be interested in her, which gave her a jolt of surprise. 'Well, we have seen each other once or twice. I just wanted to make sure that I wasn't stepping on anyone's toes before we go any further.'

Ruaridh's expression faltered. 'I see. It looks as if I've been a bit slow off the mark.'

She'd had no inkling that Ruaridh was the slightest bit interested in her romantically. But even as she felt flattered at his attention, a worry had begun to bubble within her. She hoped that this wouldn't cause any unpleasant undercurrents in the band, just when she was beginning to feel that she was making good friends.

Her sleep that night was disturbed by anxious dreams, where she found herself back on stage with Urban Hawk. The bright lights and the crowds seemed manic to her, filling her with terror as she searched frantically for a way off the stage. Waking suddenly, she lay breathless in bed in a tangle of bedclothes. Once she had registered with relief that she was safe on Arasay, Jenna began thinking about the events of the previous day. After a while she realised she felt wide awake, and looked at her clock. It was almost six o'clock. She swung her feet to the floor and headed for the window. The sky was beginning to lighten. A sudden desire for activity washed over her. Washing and dressing quickly and quietly so that she didn't disturb Morag, she scribbled a note to say that she was going for a bike ride.

Luckily the lights on the bike were operational, so she switched them on, clipped on the cycle helmet that was hanging on a hook nearby the door, and wheeled on to the path. Once in the saddle, she set off towards the sea, which was currently shrouded with mist.

It felt odd to be pedalling on the deserted single-track roads in the half-light. The mist was damp on her cheeks when she began to hear the waves breaking over the rocks, and the cries of seabirds. The fresh dampness of the morning washed away the last of her nightmare as she began to focus on the feel of the air rushing past her. Finally she could discern the seaweed on the rocks, and the sea unfurling. She imagined Jake watching the birds and tracking their movements with his lens. Would she see an otter today, she wondered? She imagined telling him once he was home, and pictured the delight on his face. A smile graced her features as she pedalled.

It was now full daylight, but the mist was still lingering. Her body had warmed with the exercise, and the red post van passed her on the road along the shoreline. The 'postie' gave her a toot and a wave, which she returned happily. It felt good to be part of this island community.

Ascending a sharp rise, Jenna was shocked to find a huge lorry bearing down on her at speed. With a cry, she turned the handlebars into the verge, but before she could reach the passing place, the vehicle was upon her, catching her rear wheel as she leaped off the bike to safety. Stunned and shaking, she found herself sprawling on the damp grass, with gravel in her palms.

'Ouch!' she muttered, picking the sharp stones from her hands. 'What a bully!' She turned her head to see if the driver had stopped, but he continued on his way without a backward glance.

She was surprised that such a large vehicle was on the tiny road, and driving at such speed, too.

Jenna gingerly clambered to her feet. Luckily she had been free of the bike when the lorry caught the wheel, and though she felt a bit bruised, she was sure she hadn't injured herself. But the bike was another matter. The rear wheel was bent. No more cycling for her this morning.

With a sigh, she took her map from her pocket and looked at how far she would have to wheel it back to Balloch. It was going to be some distance. She glanced at her watch. It was now quarter past eight. Maybe if another van came along, they could give her a lift. She set off back along the way she had come, ignoring a growing ache in her left knee.

The bike wouldn't wheel properly, but she kept on going because she knew that Morag would begin to worry if she was away too long. A couple of cars passed her going in the opposite direction, and though the drivers saluted her, they didn't stop. Then a little blue car overtook her and stopped in the next passing place.

The driver was an older woman who looked familiar, though she couldn't place her. She wound down her window as Jenna approached. 'I see you're in trouble. Are you all right?'

'Just a few scrapes, I think. But the bike is damaged so I can't ride back.' The woman opened her door and came to look at the bike. 'That's pretty bad. How did it happen?'

Jenna explained about the lorry, which made the woman exclaim in dismay. 'It must have been one from the fish farm. He should have stopped. You could have been badly hurt.'

'I wonder if he didn't see me in the mist.' Jenna noticed the sky was finally clear. It seemed an age since it had happened, and she was feeling tired. Her companion touched her arm.

'Why not leave the bike here and I'll take you home? We can phone Ruaridh and ask him to pick it up. I'm sure Morag won't mind.'

Jenna gasped. 'How did you . . . ?'

'Of course I recognise you, Jenna. You've been playing in the band, and I believe you've been seeing something of my son.' Of course — it was Jake's mother, Ailsa! Trepidation washed over her. Was she going to get another warning?

But Ailsa lips curved upwards. 'Come on, you've been shaken. Why not put the bike over there on the verge beyond the passing place.'

Jenna was relieved to be able to relax and be taken back to Balloch. Ailsa dropped her at Morag's house, and waved away her thanks, refusing to come in. 'I'm due at Arasay House. Please give my love to Morag.'

Morag was horrified by the incident, and insisted they rang the police. At Jenna's hesitation, Morag set a determined face. 'Andy McCrinan, the sergeant, will want to know about dangerous driving on Arasay.'

Jenna registered the name with incredulity. 'McCrinan? Is he a relative?'

Morag laughed as she reached for the telephone. 'You'll need to get used to the fact that a fair number of Arasay's population is still called McCrinan. We're not all related — or at least, not for a long time. This is the clan's ancestral home, after all.

The policeman, a tall athletic man in his early forties, arrived that afternoon and took a statement from Jenna. He agreed with Ailsa that the lorry was probably from the fish farm. 'I'll have a word with them. Leave it to me.'

Although he had a friendly face, Jenna judged that he could turn fierce if necessary, which reassured her. He also said he would pick up the bike and take it to Ruaridh's garage for repair.

The whole incident only served to make her realise she was part of a close-knit community now. Despite the upheaval of the day, she slept much better that night, also gratified by

Ailsa's seeming acceptance of her time
spent with Jake.

11

On the Tuesday afternoon Jenna caught the island's only bus down to the ferry terminal in time for the five o'clock passage to the mainland. She was on her way to Glasgow for her meeting with solicitor Kieron Warburton. As the bus bumped along the single-track road, she mulled over her first morning's teaching at the school. Isobel had come round the previous evening to give her some background about the school and its twenty-one pupils. Jenna would be teaching those aged between seven and eleven, which gave her a total of sixteen pupils.

'We've had some new families moving to the island in recent years,' Isobel had explained. 'People see these TV programmes about getting away from it all. Some children only stay a year or so, as the families realise it's not so easy making ends meet on a remote island like Arasay. Although we do have success stories, like the Naylor family, who moved here from England five years ago. We have three of the children in the school, and there are two more at home.'

Of course, one of her pupils was Talli, in Primary 3. Although a little more nervous of this lesson, Jenna had nothing to worry about. The little girl and her friend, Rosa Naylor, were both keen and grasped the rudiments of playing quickly. All the sessions flew by, and the thought of continuing through the term filled her with happy anticipation.

Jenna was now watching the car ferry approaching the pier. Her phone chimed twice, and she realised that the signal must have been poor that morning and that she was now in a hotspot where the texts had come through.

The first one was from her brother, Leo.

Mum told me you're in Glasgow for the next couple of nights. I'll be in Edinburgh tonight to cover the rugby international at Murrayfield, but could come over to Glasgow to join you at your hotel tomorrow night and have dinner. L x

Her heart leaping in delight, she immediately sent a reply. *Great! I'm staying at the Glasgow Shearwater Hotel. Let me know if you get booked in. Signal should be better once I'm there. J x*

Then her breath caught in her throat when she realised that the second message was from Jake.

Moved on to new location today where signal is better. Good footage of ospreys, feeling satisfied. Hope teaching went well and Talli behaved herself. Keep in touch. Jake xx

Jenna watched the ferry dock and the stream of cars and a couple of vans disembark while she thought carefully about how to phrase her reply. Excitement tickled her that he had reached out to her in the middle of his busy schedule. Maybe there wasn't anything in Kezia's claim after all. She ran her tongue over her lips at the memory of his mouth against hers.

It was late that night when she reached her hotel in Glasgow, and was glad to fall into the king-size bed. Next morning she gazed from the windows of the small business room that the young lawyer, Kieron Warburton, had hired for their meeting. By daylight they had an extensive vista of the riverbank of the Clyde.

Reassuringly, Richard had been right about Kieron — he was bright and had a good grasp of the case, and brought her up to scratch on the situation. Devon was pushing for damages under breach of contract following her refusal to return to the group. He was also disputing her right to royalties over their most popular songs, declaring that he had been the principal writer of all of these, and that she had only been a minor contributor. Luckily, Jenna had earlier versions of all the songs in her Cloud Storage, which were clearly dated. She was thankful that she'd saved subsequent versions as new files.

Kieron reckoned that Devon had no case at all over the songs, though the downside was that her royalty payments were suspended until the case was resolved. The other matter of breach of contract would have to be negotiated. 'We could possibly settle out of court for that one.'

Jenna agreed, though she worried how much this would cost her. 'I wish Devon would just replace me. But I know he's angry and wants to hurt me in some way, as he feels abandoned.'

Kieron put the last of the papers back in his briefcase. 'I heard through the grapevine that the group was in rehearsal again, and there's another female member now. Maybe we can play on that, and push that you're a minor member of the performing band. Though if we challenge the rights to the songs then that's a contradiction.'

She sighed, and pushed her chair back to stand up, stretching her stiff limbs. They had been in conference since ten o'clock that morning, and it was now almost four o'clock. They'd only had a brief break at lunchtime. 'Well, as long as you keep me informed. I'll send you the song files. I'm not giving up my rights to my own songs.'

They walked down to the lobby together, and Kieron shook her hand before leaving. He'd booked a taxi to the airport. Just as he disappeared through the glass door, Jenna felt a hand on her shoulder, and swung round.

The fair-haired young man who stood behind Jenna greeted her with a wide grin. 'Surprise! That was good timing.'

'Leo!' Jenna hugged her brother close. He looked lean and tanned, his hair cut short. 'It's so good to see you. How long has it been?'

He rolled his eyes. 'Don't ask me! I've been around the world a few times

156

since I last saw you. Let's go for a coffee.'

The evening passed all too quickly. The siblings only stopped talking when Jenna slipped up to her room to put on a clean blouse before dinner. Catching sight of herself in the full-length mirror by the door before she left the room, she was astonished to see how different she looked. Somehow she looked — happy. She couldn't have said that before she left Northumberland for Scotland. Her pixie haircut gave her a lively look, and her cheeks were pink with health, her eyes sparkling. She felt equal to standing up to Devon and his lies, and tilted her chin defiantly at her reflection with a small smile of satisfaction before going to meet her brother.

Relaxing over a drink in the bar later, Leo also complimented her on her looks. 'I must say, I prefer this style to the 'rock chick' one.'

Jenna wrinkled her nose. 'That was my public image. I'm keen to move on now.'

Leo put his arm round her shoulder. 'I can see that you're well on your way. But there's a spark in you that I've never seen before. Is there a new man in your life?'

'What makes you think that?'

'You've got a glow about you. It's not just the bracing air of the Scottish Hebrides, I'm sure. Tell me, who is he?'

'It — it's not a proper relationship yet. But I hope it might be.' Her cheeks were warm. 'Have you ever heard of a wildlife photographer called Jared — Jakob Alexander Redman, to be precise?'

Leo shook his head. 'Not my field at all. Now, if he was a sports photographer I'd be more familiar. So is he an islander?'

Jenna nodded, and outlined their story, though she missed out last week's kiss. She also explained that he was a widower with a young daughter. 'Talli's a sweetie, and I'm teaching her now in the recorder group at Arasay School.'

'It sounds as if you're smitten.'

158

A twist of apprehension caught her. 'Don't say that. It's nothing yet. Plus, I don't know if he's got something with the mother of one of Talli's friends. I'm treading carefully.'

Leo grabbed her hand. 'Don't go carefully. You have to throw yourself into your life.'

Laughing, Jenna drained her glass. 'Fat lot you know about romance! When do you have time to make any sort of relationship work?' To her surprise, he didn't laugh. 'I'm trying to remedy that now. I've been with my current girl-friend, Emily, for six months.'

Delighted at this news, she wheedled out of him that Emily was a researcher on one of the programmes at the television company where he worked. Jenna retired to her hotel room later filled with a warm glow from their meeting. There was also the promise of a lift back to Oban the next day in Leo's hire car, as her brother wasn't flying back to London until the evening.

12

It was a blustery but sunny scene that met them when they drove into Oban just before midday. As they descended the hill into the town, they had a panoramic view of the bay. A blue and white ferry was heading out of the terminal, while another smaller one sailed in. The sea in the channel between the mainland and the nearest island was blue, whipped with small white waves.

'It could be choppy out there today,' Leo said as he joined a stream of traffic winding through the town centre towards the terminal.

'It couldn't be worse than my passage in March,' Jenna replied, recalling her first encounter with Jake. There had been no more messages on her phone, which must mean that he was working hard or out of reach of a signal.

Leo pulled in as near as he could to the terminal building. He stepped out of the car with Jenna, and they hugged warmly in farewell.

'Keep me updated on how it's going with Emily. You should bring her up here in the summer.'

Leo gave a wry smile. 'I don't know if Scotland is her scene — I think she has something more exotic in mind. But maybe we'll Skype you some time, so I can introduce you.'

This reply gladdened her heart, for it seemed Leo was actually becoming serious about a girl.

'You also have to keep me in the mix about Jake,' he added.

'Well, we're not really an item yet — but I'll let you know.' With a final hug, she took her weekend bag and headed towards the terminal building to check in. She gave Leo one last wave before ducking indoors out of the wind. Despite it being April there was still a bite to the breeze. To her surprise, she found herself confronting Rachel.

'Well, that was some farewell. I thought you were interested in our attractive wildlife cameraman.' There was a slight coolness in her tone that had never been there before.

Jenna stopped, nonplussed. Did Rachel actually think that she was after every man in sight? Indignantly she corrected her. 'That's my brother, Leo. He's been up in Scotland reporting on a rugby tournament.' Rachel had the grace to look contrite. 'I'm sorry. I suppose we're all a little protective of Jake, knowing his history.'

'I need to check in.' Fighting down her indignation at Rachel's manner, Jenna began to make her way to the counter. But after a few paces she felt a hand on her arm.

'I shouldn't have jumped to conclusions,' the craft shop owner said. 'Please forgive me. I hope my faux pas won't affect our friendship.'

Jenna took her place at the back of a three-person queue, and shook her head. 'It's OK. I shouldn't have been ratty. Of course Jake's friends don't want him messed around with. You can be sure that isn't on my mind.'

'Good. Now, the ferry's nearly ready for boarding. Fancy getting some lunch on board?'

The hour and a half of the crossing flew past as the two women sat on deck exchanging news. Jenna discovered that Rachel had been visiting an art exhibition in Oban. As they came into the port at Arasay, Rachel turned to Jenna. 'I saw you the other day riding a bicycle. I don't suppose you'd like to join me for a cycle ride this weekend? I must warn you, I'm totally unfit!'

'I'd like that. It'd be good to explore the island.' Ruaridh had returned the mended bicycle in time for her to ride it to the school on Tuesday.

They agreed to meet on Sunday afternoon. Their route off the vessel took them past a lorry waiting to board that looked suspiciously like the one that had run her down, and Jenna frowned. The driver looked vaguely familiar, and it wasn't until they had reached the bus stop that she realised that it was the man who had been scrutinising Jake's Land Rover. She vowed to tell him at the first opportunity.

That evening, Jenna was just putting away the dishes from their meal when she heard the door knocker sound. When Morag opened the door, Jenna heard a deep voice.

Morag's smiling face looked round the door of the living room. 'Someone for you, Jenna! Shall I put the kettle on?' The older woman was only wearing one wrist support now, and had been managing more tasks this past week.

'Thanks, Morag. But don't strain your wrist lifting the kettle.' A flicker of excitement caught Jenna, recognising the identity of the male voice.

'I'll shout if it's too heavy.' Morag disappeared, and Jake appeared in her place.

'Hello, Jenna.' There was a depth of

warmth in his eyes which stirred her heart.

She leaped to her feet, feeling herself blushing. 'When did you get back?'

He strode across to her and took her hand. Her fingers tingled at his touch. 'Just today. We finished a day early, so I took the opportunity to pack up and come home to the women in my life.'

Could he be including her in this expression, she wondered? 'I didn't see you on the ferry — I sat on deck with Rachel.' She realised she was babbling nervously, and stopped.

With a laugh, he flung an arm round her and hugged her. 'I'm not a mirage — I got a plane from Oban. Our airport's quite serviceable, if you ever need it. I didn't take the Land Rover this time, as I was part of a large team.'

'How did the shoot go?'

His whole being came alive as he enthused about the wildlife he had been filming. Jenna was mesmerised by his descriptions, finding she could picture them in her mind.

'I can't wait to see the finished programme.'

He gave a short laugh. 'It won't be for a while yet. But I'll let you know when any of my footage is appearing on television.' Then he looked deep into her eyes. 'I'm quite busy editing this week, but next Monday morning I'm planning on some local work at an islet off Arasay. How do you fancy joining me?'

'I'd love to, thanks. Should I bring my camera?'

'Why not? I can give you some tips.'

So on the appointed morning at seven o'clock, he brought the Land Rover to her door to pick her up. Mist clung to the horizon as Jenna closed the front door softly behind her. Taking one look at the murky scene, she pulled her woolly hat on, knowing that it wouldn't be a good idea to become chilled early on.

The now familiar thrill caught her as she slipped into the seat beside him, and their eyes met with a warmth of intensity. She couldn't wait to share another wildlife adventure with him, and experience his presence once more. Jake swiftly slipped the gear stick into first gear, and powered off. Jenna pulled her gaze away from his face and looked towards the horizon.

'This really is an island of mists. Will that affect our day?'

'It may be a bit hazy. Anyway, wildlife are often less shy when the weather is poor. I've had some great shots in the rain, though of course I have to be near enough to get the images sharp.'

He told her that his mother was taking Talli to the school bus that morning, which was the reason they were able to leave so early. 'Talli wanted to come along.' He gave her a quick grin as they hurtled along the quiet single-track road, unhindered by any traffic coming the other way. 'I had to promise her a trip to the café in Balloch after school as compensation.'

Jenna laughed. 'It looks as if she knows how to twist you round her little finger.'

'She does that.' His eyes were soft with love as they drove along. 'It's tough sometimes being a sole parent, though I'm eternally grateful to my mother for letting me pursue my career, knowing that my daughter's safe with someone I trust.'

Jenna wondered briefly if it would be impossible to penetrate this tight family unit, but then her attention was caught by a large bird flying across the road ahead of them. 'What's that?'

He pulled up in a large passing place and grabbed the binoculars that were lying in the side pocket. 'Buzzard, I believe. There are golden eagles up on the hills, but it's a bit low for them here. I've never seen a sea eagle on Arasay, and anyway, that bird was too small for that.'

They set off again. After about half an hour of driving, he turned the Land Rover off the road, down a track which was unmarked. 'This is an islet, though there is a rough causeway which is good enough for a vehicle at low tide. The tide is far enough out now, and we'll be able to get back at lunchtime before it gets too deep.'

'Do many people come here?' Jenna held on to the door handle as they bumped down the narrow track and began to cross. The sea was lapping at the sides of the causeway, which was almost a hundred metres long.

'It's not advertised, because of the delicate ecology and the wildlife. We prefer to direct tourists to the other side of the island, where they can see birds nesting on the cliffs. My friend Hector takes boat trips in season. Maybe that's something you'd be interested in?'

'I like the sound of that. But I'm getting quite busy these days, what with my bookshop duties, my teaching, and the ceilidh band. Plus Rachel and I have agreed to walk or cycle together once a week. She's also wanting me to take up knitting at her craft club.'

He turned to her with a raised eyebrow. 'And how do you feel about that?'

'I'm not much of a crafty person — now music, that's different.'

At the end of the causeway Jake slowed down and turned right, heading for a rocky outcrop that overlooked the sea. They went up a short rise, then dropped down towards a bay where there were three ruined buildings. 'What's happening when Craig's fit enough to return to the band?'

'I've played my flute in one or two numbers, and Ruaridh has suggested that I do that permanently, but it really depends on how the others feel. After all, it would mean splitting the fees between four rather than three.'

'Another instrument would surely bring more character to the band. But you're right, it will dilute the profits, unless you can find another way of generating some income.'

'I've been having some ideas about doing a recording. Visitors often ask for a CD, and I have some knowledge of how to go about it from my time in the music industry.'

He nodded. 'That sounds like a good idea.' He pulled up behind a low hummock at some distance from the ruins. 'Now, I need to remind you about Talli's rule.'

Jenna raised her eyebrows. 'What's that?'

'Something I've taught my daughter right from her earliest times on a shoot with me. Keep quiet, don't disturb the wildlife.'

With a flash of a grin, she nodded.

Jake showed her that the hummock was in fact a cleverly hidden hide, and he gave her some equipment to carry into it. It was sheltered inside, with a good view of the bay. Jenna settled herself in the niche that he indicated for her, and she sat patiently with her camera on her lap as she watched him set up a video camera on a tripod.

Once it was all in place, he grabbed a small plastic stool that was tucked in one corner, and hunkered down, whispering to her that during these few hours the otters might come out to fish, as low tide was a good time to spot them. Though Jenna enjoyed watching Jake at work, she pulled her gaze away and put her attention on the seabirds coming in to feed. She had studied a book of local wildlife before coming, and so recognised oyster catchers, kittiwakes, black headed gulls and sanderlings flying in and out, or foraging in the shallow waters and the sand. The chattering of their calls filled the air, meaning that the observers could communicate quietly without worrying about disturbing the birds. There were also the spare black shapes of cormorants on a rock further away.

Jake set up her camera for the conditions of light, explaining what he was doing to capture the best shots. He had also loaned her a more powerful zoom lens which she found thrilling to use. It was fantastic to be able to get really close shots and see the intricate detail of the birds' behaviour. After the first hour, Jenna took fewer photos, but attached her own lens to snap some of

Jake as he was concentrating. It was so peaceful here with him, and she felt that he was opening himself to her in allowing her to share his work.

At half past eleven, he looked at his watch, and sighed. 'I'm disappointed you didn't get the chance to see an otter today. There's a holt up that hill, and I've frequently seen them in conditions like this. I'm going down carefully to take a look, because it's a few months now since I found any here.'

Jenna watched him creep up the hill, keeping a low profile and almost flat at the final few metres. While examining it closely, he even pulled back some grass in a few places. He returned, shaking his head with a grim expression.

'It's deserted, and it looks as if someone's been poking around the entrances to the holt. I hope desperately that no-one has hurt the otters. Although why anyone should dream of disturbing them, I don't know.'

Their mood was more sombre as

they cleared up and left the islet to drive back to Balloch. Jenna could almost feel his anxiety radiating off him as he drove. Obviously the disturbance to the wildlife of the island had worried him. She contented herself with searching each bay they passed for a sight of the otters, but in vain.

Finally they approached the bookshop and Jenna's house. 'Morag will be pleased with me,' he said in a brighter tone. 'Bringing you home for lunch with ten minutes to spare.'

Jenna thanked him for lending her the telephoto lens. 'I can't wait to download my pictures, but I'll need to wait until this evening now.'

'Let me know how they turn out. You can show me them later in the week.' He placed a hand on her upper arm and grazed her lips with his. It made her shiver with pleasure, and she longed for a more lingering farewell, but obviously he was eager to get away. As she waved at the departing vehicle, her emotions were in a pleasant turmoil. It had been a good morning, and they'd shared something special. Were they really at the start of a proper relationship?

13

Jenna paused for a brief moment in front of the sign that said Tala Baile. She ran the Gaelic words over her tongue, savouring the sounds. It sounded so much more romantic than 'Village Hall', the translation printed underneath. The key was cold and hard in her hand as she darted round to the side. She'd requested to borrow it from Ruaridh under the pretext of practising on the piano, but had another motive as well. Once inside, she whipped off the cover from the digital instrument and plugged it in, her breath short with delicious anticipation.

Tucked inside her book of Scottish ceilidh tunes were a few sheets of manuscript with some sketched notes, and hastily scribbled words down the sides. These snatches of tunes had begun to seed in her mind as she walked and cycled round the island, or gazed from her bedroom window in the long summer evenings when she was practising her flute. She wanted to experiment with harmonies, and allow the words and melodies to flow and develop.

Soon she was immersed in her music, and a song was beginning to take shape. She jotted down the chord symbols quickly. It felt as if only a few minutes had passed before she heard the side door open again, and she quickly pushed the manuscript sheets into the ceilidh book and began to play a Scottish number.

'Hello, Jenna!'

Her fingers paused on the keys when she realised that it was Craig, his accordion case under his arm. Her heart sank. Was her time in the band over?

She pasted a welcoming smile on her face. 'Hello, Craig. How are you?'

He walked over to her and placed the

case on a nearby table. 'Much improved, thanks. I'm going to try out a number with the band today, to see how I get on. But I won't be up to scratch for a while yet. I hope you'll continue to play.'

Relief flooded her. 'I can't deny that I've really enjoyed being a part of the band.'

'Why not join in with your flute when I'm playing? I thought it sounded really good last week. It fills out the sound.'

Astonished, she let her hands drop into her lap. 'Well, that's really kind, Craig. I'd love to keep it up. As long as the others don't mind.'

'Of course we don't.' Hamish's voice broke in. 'We're all for it.' He was approaching them with his fiddle case, Ruaridh on his heels.

Jenna's heart soared at being asked to stay in the band. By the end of May, Craig was returning to full strength, and Jenna was further surprised when the men told her they had decided that the piano would sound good for Ruaridh's songs. It felt so good to have an outlet for her music. It inspired her to finish her song, and begin another.

The evenings were stretching out and more visitors were coming to Arasay. Jake was filming and photographing round the island in between the occasional few days away on the mainland. He managed to send her texts whenever he could. When he was home they telephoned every day, and he dropped in to see her frequently. They also had a successful excursion where they were rewarded with sightings of a mother otter and cub on the rocks, playing with a fish they had caught. With Jake's telephoto lens Jenna took some good photos, of which she was very proud.

He invited her to come with him to a talk he was giving on a neighbouring island one Friday. 'I'll call for you as soon as the bookshop closes, if Morag doesn't mind. Wear something warm — we're going in Hecky's boat. But maybe something a bit more dressy underneath, as I'd like to take you to a special restaurant afterwards.'

Excitement welled up inside her. To be whisked off by sea, entertained, then wined and dined, sounded like a perfect date to her. Luckily the Hebridean islands were in the midst of a few days of high pressure, so it was a deliciously balmy evening. Jenna had recently bought on the internet a multi-coloured jacket in black and white with added accents of yellow and turquoise, which she wore over a black gauzy sleeveless top and some new black skinny jeans. On top she had her winter padded jacket to keep out the wind.

The boat was moored at a small jetty on the north east of Arasay. There was a sign advertising wildlife tours on Tuesdays and Thursdays during the summer months, and a Friday trip to Staffa to see the legendary Fingal's Cave. The vessel looked as if it would take about twelve passengers. There was a small cabin, with ranks of outdoor seats at the rear. A figure appeared from inside the boat at the sound of their approach.

Jake called out as they walked down the jetty. 'Hello, Hecky! All set?'

The sailor looked to be about seventy years old, his features lined from days spent at sea. His teeth flashed white in his face as he grinned and replied, 'Aye, Jakob. Ready for the off!'

'Jenna, meet Hector McPhee, who set me on the path to fame and fortune. I spent much of my youth on his boat, photographing dolphins and whales, and spotting seabirds in between helping out on the tours.'

'Get away with you,' the other man growled, holding out a gnarled hand to grasp Jenna's. 'Pleased to meet you, miss. Hope you like the sea — it can get a bit choppy on a small boat.'

Jenna instinctively smiled back at his friendly greeting. 'I don't mind as long as I have something to hold on to. I've done some sailing off the coast of Northumberland in the past with my dad.'

'Aye, well, that's good. Jump aboard.'

Jake took her hand and helped her climb into the boat. Hecky untethered the rope from the jetty, and tossed it to Jake before climbing in behind them. He handed them both life jackets to put on, then they took their seats in the rear of the vessel. In the wheelhouse, Hecky sprang the engine to life. Soon they were motoring out of the little bay, the boat beginning to leap over the waves as they gathered speed.

It was an exhilarating journey, watching Arasay recede behind them, passing islets inhabited by cormorants and gulls. Jake handed Jenna a powerful set of binoculars, pointing out some seals basking on rocks in the approach to the neighbouring island where they were to land. With delight, she adjusted the focus and gazed at the sleek dark, mammals observing the boat passing by. White gannets with black-tipped wings swooped and dived into the water around them. Finally the boat entered a small inlet, and its speed dropped.

Jenna removed the hood of her jacket which had been protecting her from the breeze, and took a deep breath of the sea air.

'It feels so good to fill my lungs with such freshness,' she said, closing her eyes and savouring it. Jake put his arm round her shoulder and hugged her. 'You've turned out to be quite an outdoor girl, Jenna. I wasn't expecting that when I first met you.'

Her eyes opened quickly, studying his face. 'Really? Why was that?'

'Well, when you told me that you'd worked in the music business in London, I thought you'd miss the big city.'

A twist of guilt inside her made her wonder if this was the opportunity to reveal her past identity. But they were approaching a small jetty, and now wasn't the moment to bare her heart. Maybe later. 'I love it here,' was all she said as he slipped away from her to take the rope and jump ashore to moor the vessel firmly.

A large SUV was waiting nearby. A dark-haired woman who looked to be in her forties opened the door and called out a greeting. 'Do you need a hand with anything?'

'No thanks, Cathy. We've got it all.' Jake was carrying a box of his books, while Jenna had a laptop case and a tube containing posters of his photos for display. It only took five minutes to drive to the venue in the local hall. Hecky came along with them, but declined to join them, saying he would spend the evening at the nearby hotel bar catching up with his local friends.

'The islands are like a small neighbourhood, especially amongst the boat owners. He's probably known them for fifty years or more,' Jake said as they entered the hall. It didn't take him long to set up, and connect the laptop containing his presentation to the hall's system. Spectators began arriving soon after, and he started his talk at seven o'clock. Jenna was fascinated to hear him speak, not just about the wildlife of

Arasay and the other islands, but also some insights into his filming techniques. The evening ended with some questions, many from keen photographers discussing tips of the trade. Finally they were packed up at eight-fifteen.

Jake put an arm round her and thanked her for her patience. 'I've booked a table at a local restaurant, and Cathy is going to drop us off. Hecky's getting a lift back to the boat from one of his mates, and we'll get a taxi when we're done.

When Cathy drove them down to the spit of land where the hotel was situated, Jenna's eyes widened with surprise to see a sprawling, modern building made up of modules faced with sandy coloured stone and extensive glass windows on the sides which faced the sea. The sun was still quite high due to their northern latitude. The wind had died down, and it had turned into one of those balmy warm summer evenings that were so peaceful on the west of Scotland. Cathy wished them a good meal, thanking Jake once more for the talk, and drove off, leaving them to their evening together.

Their table in the restaurant looked out to sea from one of the vast windows. In the distance there were shapes of nearby islands. The maitre d' greeted Jake with pleasure, obviously familiar with him, but once they were shown to their table, they were left discreetly in peace.

Conversation flowed, but all at once she became aware that Jake was mulling over something. He gazed into his wine glass, swirling the liquid around for a few seconds before taking a mouthful. Then he looked her straight in the eyes. 'Jenna, you know about my past, and my marriage to Savannah — but I know so little about your past life, your previous relationships.'

Something twisted in her chest, and she laid down her glass so that he wouldn't see her hands shaking. Not now! She couldn't tell him about Urban

Hawk now, and disturb the beautiful intimacy of the evening. What's more, the tables around them had filled up, and someone might overhear her. But she had to say something. She took a deep breath. 'I was in a relationship with someone I worked with. We were together a few years, but in the end it didn't last.'

Jake nodded softly. 'What happened?'

Heart thudding, she shrugged. 'He changed — he was boyish and enthusiastic when we met, but as he matured our values began to differ. He was only interested in making money. I think the breakdown of our relationship contributed to my illness, and he wasn't very supportive.'

'What was he called?'

Jenna paused, wondering if she should make up a name. But in the end she said, 'Niall.'

But the name clearly meant nothing to Jake. After all, Niall Devon had been known by his surname in the band. The waiter arrived to remove their plates, and offered them the dessert menu. The moment passed, and they began to talk about other matters. Jenna wondered if she would regret not taking that opportunity to open up, but decided to save it for another time.

A pink hue began to spread over the sky, and the few clouds that stretched across the atmosphere gradually deepened into red. After their meal they walked down to the shore.

'This is so beautiful,' Jenna sighed.

Jake's arm was round her shoulder. 'And so are you,' he said as he pulled her closer and covered her mouth with his own.

It was a perfect moment. Tasting his lips, feeling her whole body tingling and alive, as if she was melting against this tall, strong man, she wished it could go on for ever. With reluctance she finally let him draw apart from her, knowing that their taxi was due to take them back to the boat. Sailing back to Arasay was blissful, sitting in peaceful silence in the back of the boat with Jake's arm round her, holding his other hand and content in his company. The sky darkened into deep blue, and stars began to twinkle in the canopy above them. It formed a comforting arc above them for their sea journey.

As they were about to enter the bay where Hecky tethered his boat, the older man called out to Jake from the cabin. 'Look yonder. Is that a boat with no lights over there?'

Jake's head snapped up from where it was resting against Jenna's hair. She immediately roused, her heart beginning to pound at the disturbance. Jake released her from his gentle hold, and the cold air invaded her space without his body to keep her warm. Quickly he grasped the binoculars that were stowed at the mouth of the cabin, and raised them to his eyes.

At that moment Hecky gave a shout and their boat lurched violently to one side, throwing Jenna and Jake on to the deck. The breath knocked out of her, Jenna looked up in alarm and saw a large dark shape passing by the bow of the boat.

'Are you OK?' Jake was at her side instantly.

'Yes,' she gasped, pulling herself back on to the seat. Her shoulder had taken a blow, but it wasn't anything serious. 'Did that boat deliberately come straight at us?'

'It looks like it.' Jake touched her gently before grabbing the binoculars. Back at the rail, he trained them on the shape that had almost rammed them as it receded into the darkness.

'Has that boat gone?' Jenna asked, her heart rate beginning to return to normal.

Jake lowered the binoculars. 'I believe so. It's not displaying any lights, but there was enough of a glow in the sky for me to see the shape disappearing off to the west. I've lost sight of the smaller vessel without lights that Hecky spotted nearer the shore.'

'Surely that's against the code of conduct for sea vessels?'

'Something illegal going on!' Hecky called from the cabin. 'I'm contacting the coastguard.' Jake nodded, though he didn't move from his lookout point. 'Any boat that sails without lights and deliberately tries to ram another is up to no good. We're lucky that Hecky has such quick reactions and managed to get us out of the way.'

Once they had motored into the inlet by Hecky's cottage, Jake jumped ashore and moored up securely. The older man emerged from the cabin, his mouth set into a hard line. 'I've had word over the radio that the rogue boats had disabled their satellite signature, so they aren't on record. I don't know if the coastguard will get out here in time to catch them, especially as they won't be able to detect their positions.'

'Why would they want to hide?' Jenna asked Jake once they had taken their leave of Hecky and were returning to the Land Rover.

'Plenty of reasons — illegal fishing and smuggling, for a start.' He put his arm round her shoulders. 'I'm sorry that it spoiled the evening.'

They stood still beside the vehicle and waved to Hecky, who was tramping up the rise to his cottage. 'I won't let it ruin my evening,' she declared. 'I've enjoyed it so much. It was wonderful being out on the sea, then hearing your talk, sharing the meal and the beautiful sunset with you. That last incident was only brief.'

'Good.' He brushed his lips over hers. As soon as they were back on the road, he covered her hand with his while he steered the car one-handed. But it took Jenna a lot of willpower to try and banish the fright she had felt when the other boat had come at them. It was disturbing to think that there were bad things happening in this remote, peaceful place.

14

Jake was away on a shoot for the next couple of weeks. Jenna was glad of the rush of work that came with the end of the school term, as well as the increasing business in the bookshop, to take her mind off how much she was missing him. They opened the bookshop every afternoon except Sunday during the tourist season, and she was surprised at how busy the premises became. During this time, deliveries were larger for them and the other small businesses, and sometimes Ruaridh brought along Grant Fenton from the garage to help unload the boxes. Despite his friendliness, Jenna found Fenton's smile sinister as it never seemed to reach his eyes. She was always relieved when he left. Like many local men he had several jobs on the island, including driving lorries for the fish farm.

There was a school performance in

the village hall during the last week of term. It was just past midsummer's day, which was the theme of the concert. It was based around a play telling the story of a local folk tale through dancing, song and reciting. Jenna's six most confident pupils (including Talli) gave a performance on recorder, while Jenna herself played the flute with them.

The whole concert was just over an hour, and finished with soft drinks and cupcakes. Isobel approached Jenna while she was putting away her flute and chatting with two mothers, and handed her a glass of orange squash.

Jenna thanked her as she took the drink. 'My throat feels really dry now — but I'm so pleased with the kids.'

Isobel smiled. 'They were marvellous. I hope you'll continue to teach next term. I know that Morag is managing much better now, and I don't know what your plans are.'

After taking a quick sip and savouring the cool liquid soothing her throat,

Jenna replied, 'I'd love to stay on the island, at least until Christmas. I need to see if I can make a living here, enough to rent somewhere of my own, because I don't want to impose myself on Morag.' She also knew that it could depend on how her court hearing went, and whether she would still have an income from her songs for Urban Hawk.

'Good.' Isobel was unable to continue the conversation because another parent came up to chat, and she was whisked away. After putting her flute in her bag, Jenna straightened up and found herself looking into the amber eyes that so often haunted her dreams. 'I'm pleased to hear that you're planning on staying, Miss Davidson,' Jake told her gravely, with a twinkle in his eyes.

Her face flaming, she licked her lips. 'I didn't realise you were so close that you could overhear me.' She had been aware of him sitting at the back with his mother during the performance, which had added to her nerves. He picked up the music on her stand and handed it to her so she could pack it in a box. 'I'm just a proud parent like any other, wanting to talk to the teacher who inspired my daughter to do well.'

'That group has learned very quickly. They're my star pupils — but I'm so pleased with all of the children. I hope that was clear to everyone who was listening.'

'It was.' He leaned closer so that his next words couldn't be overheard. 'I'd like to ask you, Miss Davidson, if you would like to come with us to the Gobhar Castle Highland Show after the end of term. It's on the Sunday, so you don't need to worry about the book-shop.'

Delighted, a quick acceptance sprung to her lips. Then she frowned. 'It wouldn't be very polite of me to abandon Morag. We usually cook Sunday dinner together.'

'No problem — by 'us' I was meaning Talli and my mother, so Morag is invited as well.'

'That sounds great. I'll look forward to it.' Then she added, 'Did you hear any more about the boats without lights?'

His expression clouded as he shook his head. 'Andy McCrinan told me that the local coastguard went out as soon as Hecky reported the incident, but they had disappeared. But it's been noted and they know they have to be on their guard.'

Jenna had to be satisfied with that. Hopefully they would catch the culprits sometime.

The single-track road along the north east side of Arasay was quite busy that Sunday as the five of them travelled in the Land Rover. Jake was constantly having to pull in to allow another car to pass in the opposite direction. They reached the turn-off for Gobhar Castle after half an hour of driving. Jenna had heard about this fifteenth-century ruin, but had never visited it.

'Welcome to your ancestral home!'

Jake announced as he turned on to the track towards a thicket of trees, beyond which a ruined tower was visible, and some overgrown walls.

Morag laughed. 'Well, if it's our ancestral home, it's yours as well.'

'I hardly feel like a McCrinan,' Ailsa murmured. 'It's a good century since the male line ran out on our side. We're McCrinan-Hartleys.'

Jenna watched eagerly through the trees for her first proper view of Gobhar Castle. They emerged into bright daylight and a scene of bustling activity. A steward directed them to a parking place behind one crumbled wall. The car park was filling up fast. People of all ages, some wearing kilts, were heading towards a gap in the tall hedge beneath the wall.

'Where's your kilt?' Jenna asked Jake under her breath as they followed the crowd.

He grinned. 'I'm not taking part in the Highland dancing, or tossing the caber, though I might join in the tug o' war if I'm needed.'

'I'll look forward to that,' she replied with a twinkle. It was all she had imagined — bagpipes, highland dancing, caber tossing, and livestock. Talli and her little friend Rosa showed one of the Naylors' lambs and to their delight were rewarded with a rosette for second place. After lunch Ailsa and Morag enjoyed the flower tent, while Jake and Jenna examined the new history boards erected by the ruins. Rosa's mum, Zoe, took the girls to watch the pony races.

The final event, the tug o' war, was scheduled for later in the afternoon, and Jake signed up for one of the teams. When the time approached, he and Jenna went to collect Talli from the equestrian field. Jenna spotted Talli, holding the lead of a little black and white dog, while Rosa tossed a ball for the animal to catch. Talli called out, 'Daddy, come and play with us!'

'Who's this wee guy?' Jake bent down to fondle the head of the friendly little

199

terrier, who came to meet him with tail
wagging.

'That's MacTavish,' Rosa stated.

'He's Grant's dog,' Talli added.

'Not Grant Fenton?' Jenna said,
uneasiness rising in her.

'Yes, he brings MacTavish to our
beach for walks. He lets me play with
him there, so he's a friend of mine.'

'You mean Grant Fenton's a friend of
yours?' Jake uttered sharply.

'No, silly Daddy. MacTavish is my
friend. Grant's a man, he's not my
friend.'

Jake fondled Talli's silky hair. His face
was pinched with worry. 'I'm glad to
hear that. I don't think Grant Fenton is
a particularly nice person, even if you
like his dog. You must promise me not
to speak with him again, or play with
his dog, especially if I'm not around.
Promise?'

Talli looked at the ground at this
rebuke, and nodded miserably. Jake
sighed and pulled her into his arms,
hugging her gently. 'I think it's time for

you to return MacTavish to his owner.' He flashed an intense look at Jenna, who nodded in agreement. Clearly he was fuming, but not wanting to alarm his blameless daughter.

'Look, he's over there.' Rosa took the lead from Talli's reluctant hands and led the dog away.

'We were having such fun.' Talli's eyes were brimming with tears. He gave her a confident smile. 'It's time for the tug o' war, and you promised you would cheer me on. That's only fair, seeing as I cheered you on earlier.'

Talli nodded gravely. 'I'd really love a dog of my own, like MacTavish. He's such good fun.'

Jake shook his head. 'We talked about this before, Talli. It's too difficult when I'm away so often, and it's not fair to ask Granny Ailsa to take responsibility for a dog. We'll think about it when you're old enough to look after one yourself.'

Misery lodged on the child's face. 'Well, if I can't have a dog, maybe I could have a wee brother or sister instead. Rosa's baby sister is lovely.' The baby was eighteen months old.

Jake gave a strange choked laugh. 'Oh, Talli, we've talked about this as well. Babies need a mummy, so that's just not possible while it's just you and me.'

Jenna couldn't look at him, her heart beating faster at these words. Could she see a future as the mother of his children? He probably wouldn't want anyone to intrude in his happy family, and she didn't want him to think that she was being pushy and looking too far ahead. Just take it slowly, she told herself. The difficult moment passed once they reached the teams assembling for the tug o' war. Andy McCrinan the policeman gave them a wave.

'Hello Jake, you're with us. Come on!'

Jake kissed the top of Talli's head and flung a smile back to Jenna before heading off to join them. 'Make sure I can hear you shouting for my team!' he called back.

Talli, quite unbidden, slipped her hand into Jenna's. Jenna, still worried about the revelation that Fenton had been insinuating himself into the affections of the child, squeezed Talli's fingers. By the time Ailsa and Morag joined them, the teams had lined up. Jake tossed them a glance with a grin, but soon he was concentrating hard, digging his heels into the soft earth like the others on his end of the rope as they pulled against the strength of the opposition. It was a close run competition, but with a huge effort, and encouraging shouts from the spectators, Jake's team managed to edge their way backwards. By this time the others had run out of strength, and they were pulled off their feet. Jenna and Talli shrieked with delight. Jake staggered towards them rather unsteadily, his face split with a satisfied grin.

'Daddy, you were ace! I knew you'd win!'

Jake picked Talli up and swung her round, kissing her soundly. 'I had a good team, poppet.'

He flung his free arm round Jenna's shoulders. 'Did you enjoy that? The sight of good Scottish male muscle?'

Jenna laughed. 'There was a bit of female Scottish muscle too, remember! But it was great! Congratulations.'

By the time Jake slaked his thirst in the refreshment tent, it was time to leave. As they drove home, Jenna allowed herself to believe that she was becoming closer to his family.

15

Two weeks later it was the ten-day Arasay summer festival. Events included whisky tasting with Highland dancing at Gobhar Castle, a boat race round the island, and the opening of a new exhibition at the little museum. There was also a visiting band, Island Fiddles, which consisted of four fiddle players with a drum kit and double bass player. This up-and-coming young band presented traditional music with a rock twist, and performed at various locations all over Arasay. The island's Gaelic choir gave a concert at the church on each Sunday evening, plus an open air performance on the Wednesday, which was luckily a dry evening. Morag announced that she felt she was back into the swing of her life at long last, which was good to hear, but made Jenna question her motives for staying.

After the festival, Jake left for his latest assignment on the Sunday lunchtime ferry, and Ailsa invited Jenna to join her and Talli on Gobhar beach that afternoon.

'It'll help take her mind off her daddy leaving, if you're here. Plus it would be nice for us all to get to know each other better.'

This gave Jenna a thrill. It looked as if she was being accepted by both Jake's mother and daughter. 'I'd love to, thanks.'

Ailsa drove them past Gobhar Castle to the island's largest beach. Jenna had vague recollections of visiting it as a child, but nothing prepared her for the view when they turned off to the track that led down to the sands.

She opened the car door and walked to the viewpoint. Raising a hand to shield her eyes from the sun, she gazed over the golden expanse of sand. 'I don't remember it being so magnificent. It's breathtaking.'

There were a few other groups of

people on the wide beach. Some of them were braving the waves, but Ailsa directed them to a sheltered inlet with some tall rocks that protected them from the wind, where they unfolded their chairs.

'It's good to be with someone with local knowledge,' Jenna said. 'You can really feel the heat of the sun now we're out of the wind.'

Talli laid her towel on the sand. 'This is our special place. Daddy has been teaching me to swim, and Granny said you would help me today.'

'I realise now why you asked me if I could swim,' Jenna protested to Ailsa. 'It's a fix up!'

Unable to conceal her mirth, Ailsa held up her hands. 'My years of swimming in the sea are long gone!' She gave a shudder. 'You'll find it deep enough in the pool for Talli, and we've never let her do anything other than paddle in the sea.'

They spent a happy half hour in their swimsuits splashing in the water, at the end of which the little girl was managing to cross most of the pool by herself. Talli then began building a sandcastle. In a low voice, so that her granddaughter wouldn't hear, Ailsa thanked Jenna. 'She's never swum unassisted before. I know she was ready, but it helped having someone else here — she wanted to prove herself to you.'

It gave Jenna a warm feeling to have been part of a step in Jake's daughter's life. She was beginning to relax in the company of his family.

Ailsa went on. 'Jake tells me you had a job in music in London. That must have been exciting. It's very quiet here in comparison.'

Jenna's mouth became dry as she tried to frame her answer in the right way. 'London was all right for a while. But I grew up on the Northumberland coast. I love the outdoors. I was totally overworked in my job, and I paid the price with my health. After recuperating from pneumonia at my parents' home, I realised that the fast life had lost its lustre. Coming to Arasay turned out to be exactly right for me. I love it here.'

Ailsa continued to watch Talli while she spoke. 'That may be all right for a short time, but it's different living here all year round. We get some severe winter storms, and the days are short as we go into the solstice. We can't just escape to 'civilisation' whenever we want. Sometimes the ferries don't run if the weather's bad.'

Jenna wanted to convince Aisla that she was serious. 'I'm going to stay on and help Morag run the bookshop. I have my teaching at the school, which I adore. I plan to get a digital piano of my own, and maybe there might be interest in a few lessons from the islanders.'

Ailsa turned to her, the expression on her face unfathomable. 'Well, it sounds as if you've got it all worked out. Let's see if you still feel the same when you've experienced an Arasay winter. Savannah couldn't stand it. I hope you won't get your hopes up — or anyone else's for that matter.'

Jenna swallowed her irritation at being compared with Jake's dead wife, realising that Ailsa was being protective of her son and granddaughter. She forced herself to smile. 'I'm not Savannah. I'm a totally different person.'

Ailsa paused for a few moments before replying with a more relaxed expression. 'Yes, you are.' Then she picked up her flask. 'Coffee?'

The heavy atmosphere cleared as they talked of other matters. Jenna asked Ailsa about growing up on the island, how different it was for her being the daughter of the Laird.

'I spent a few years at the primary school, as my father was keen that we shouldn't be elitist and separated from the islanders. I'm glad I did — I made lots of friends, and it meant that I felt a real part of Arasay. My brother did too. David felt comfortable coming back here to live in Arasay House and run the estate.'

By three o'clock the tide was encroaching on their area, so they went back to the Redman house. Jenna stayed until five o'clock, then cycled home. What Ailsa had said about Savannah preyed on her mind, and she asked Morag what she remembered about her.

Her great aunt nodded. 'I used to see Jake's wife around the island, and she was totally unlike you — tall, with masses of dark wavy hair, and sultry eyes. Plus she had a permanently bored look, it seemed to me.'

'Well, I don't know whether to be flattered or insulted,' Jenna joked.

'I would have thought that he would want someone completely different after the way she treated him. I reckon Savannah pined for city life and didn't like being at home with a baby. I suppose that Jake thought they could save their marriage by going back to America. But I get the impression it wasn't too successful.'

Jenna didn't reply, lost in her own

thoughts. Could she really be the type of person Jake was looking for? Certainly, he had taken her emotions by storm. Just thinking of him with his camera intently studying wildlife, or straining his muscles at the tug o' war, or tenderly kissing his little girl, made her weak at the knees.

He'd warned her before he went that he would be in the Himalayas on the trail of snow leopards, and contact would be difficult. It was a delight when, on the Tuesday, he called her via satellite phone. His euphoria at having filmed some useful footage of these elusive animals was uplifting. It felt good that he was thinking of her.

'I miss you,' he said just before he rang off.

Her heart flipped. 'I miss you too. I'm looking forward to hearing all about your trip when you come home.'

There was to be a preliminary hearing of her court case the following month, which thankfully Jenna didn't have to attend. Then the date for the main event would be set. Her solicitor had contacted her with offers from Devon to settle out of court over the songs. Jenna had refused them all, as she would have to give up most of her rights and that would make her considerably out of pocket. She wanted to make sure that she would still get her full royalties from performances of her songs and sales of the Urban Hawk recordings. That would give her a financial cushion for her proposed new life on Arasay.

In the meantime, Jenna immersed herself in music. She was going to the village hall most days to work on her new songs. They were developing in a totally new style, with strong folk elements that had never been in her previous work. The moods of the island, with its still, clear mornings, misty days, dark rain-laden clouds and evenings when the red sun sank right into the sea, had stirred her creative juices as nothing else had done. Plus the strong emotions she was experiencing were pouring out into her music. It was a torture to her when the village hall wasn't free, and she had to try and vocalise at home or play the melodies on her flute, or write them into the music app. The sooner she found her own place and could buy a digital piano, it would be so much more fulfilling.

Jenna was preparing to go out for a cycle ride with Rachel on the following Sunday morning, when the house telephone shrilled. Morag answered it, and called upstairs.

'Jenna, it's for you!'

Grabbing her jacket and trainers, she hurried down, and regarded Morag with a quizzical look as she took the receiver. Morag mouthed the word, 'Ailsa'.

'Jenna, is that you?' Ailsa's voice sounded strange, rather wobbly.

'Yes, I'm here, Ailsa. What's wrong?'

'I'm so sorry to trouble you, but I'm not well, I've had a dreadful night with earache, and I just don't feel that I can cope with looking after Talli. Her friend Rosa's mum has taken their family to visit cousins in England, and Kezia is also away. I wonder if I could beg your help. Could you keep an eye on Talli for a day or two?'

Jenna managed to stammer, 'Of course, I'd be glad to help. Do you think she'll mind being left with me on my own?' What she really meant was, Can I look after this child on my own? Her mouth was dry.

'Thanks Jenna. Don't worry, I've asked Talli, and she said she'd like to spend a couple of days with you. Would you be able to cycle over?'

'Yes, I'll be over as soon as I've packed a bag. I'm so sorry you're not well. Have you contacted the surgery?'

'Yes, Ian Drummond is coming out to see me, so hopefully he'll give me something to clear it up. It was painful yesterday, but overnight it has been really unbearable, and I just want to lie down.'

They rang off, and Jenna explained

the situation to Morag before rushing back upstairs to stuff some clothes into a rucksack. She also added her flute, recorder, and some music.

She hugged Morag at the door. 'Will you be able to find someone to help you in the bookshop tomorrow and Tuesday? I feel bad having to leave you in the lurch.'

Morag shushed her concerns. 'That wee girl is more important than the bookshop. I'll see if Isobel can help out, as she's back from her holiday now. Caitlin, my former assistant, may be able to come for an hour or two as well. She said she'd be happy to fill in anytime as her neighbour has offered to look after wee Morgan. Now, off you go, and I'll telephone Rachel to let her know you're not able to join her today.'

'Thanks! I'd completely forgotten about Rachel. Tell her I'll text when I have a moment.' Her nerves were beginning to kick in by the time she had cycled to the Redman house. Ailsa's car was outside the house, as well as an unfamiliar dark grey car. Ian Drummond, the doctor, opened the door. His sandy hair was standing up on end as if he had been running his hands through it. He gave her a welcoming smile and ushered her in.

'Here's your angel of mercy, Talli! Now Granny can go home to have a good sleep.'

Ailsa was sitting on the settee in the living room with a tearful Talli tucked into her embrace beside her. The child looked up and said tremulously, 'But I don't want Granny to go away! She always takes care of me when Daddy's working.'

Ailsa, her face white and her lips bloodless, forced a smile and hugged Talli. 'I'll soon be right as rain, don't you worry. I'm only down the road at my little house, so I'll telephone you when I've had a rest, and you can tell me all that you've been doing with Jenna. You'll have a lovely time — you know that Daddy likes her, and you've done some fun things with her already.'

Jenna's pulse was racing at such an unfamiliar situation. She added brightly, 'I've brought my recorder and flute, so we can play some music, and then we can have some games. Granny will be better before you know it, and in the meantime, we'll have a good time.'

Talli nodded solemnly, as if uncertain, but came to take Jenna's hand. Before Ailsa left with Ian, she kissed her granddaughter, and looked up at Jenna. 'There's enough food in the fridge for tonight and tomorrow, but you'll need to do some shopping by Tuesday. My neighbour Peter will give you a lift into Balloch. I've left his number.'

'Don't worry, we'll be fine,' Jenna said with more confidence than she felt. It sounded as if she would need to stay longer than two days. They stood at the door waving as Ian drove Ailsa down to her cottage. Then she turned to the little girl, and asked what she would like to do.

'I don't know,' Talli said in a small voice. Jenna realised that she was going to have to be the adult and take charge. She suggested that they play a game, and when the girl showed her a box full of toys and games, Jenna selected some skittles, thinking that something active would take Talli's mind off the upset to her secure life. It must be very unsettling, she surmised, to be abandoned by both father and grandmother unexpectedly, and thrust into the care of a relative stranger.

Gradually Talli relaxed, and began to enjoy the activity. They filled the rest of the day with a walk down to the seashore, and some television.

Ailsa telephoned in the early evening to say that she had had a good sleep, and was taking the medicine that Ian had prescribed for her. She spoke briefly with Talli. There was no communication from Jake that day, which disappointed Jenna, as it would have been a comfort for the child — and for her, too. He must be out of range of a signal.

Talli showed her the normal bedtime

ritual, which Jenna made sure she complied with. They read a story together, but Jenna sensed that the little girl was uneasy. Once or twice her eyes began to close, but then they snapped open as she struggled to keep away sleep.

They reached the end of the chapter, and Jenna closed the book, a little knot of anxiety inside her. 'How about trying to sleep now?'

Talli looked at her with her small brow furrowed. 'Is Granny going to die?'

'Oh, darling, of course not!' Impulsively, Jenna reached out and enveloped her in a firm hug, feeling a sob convulse the little body in her arms. 'Granny just has a poorly ear, and she's going to be fine very soon with the medicine that the doctor gave her.'

Talli clung to her. 'I miss Daddy,' a small muffled voice came from the depths of Jenna's cardigan.

'I know,' Jenna said softly, and kissed the top of her head. 'But you're safe with me, and Granny's just down the road. We'll call in to see how she is tomorrow, and I'm sure Daddy will be able to telephone too. Just think of him filming the animals.' She leaned back and looked into Talli's face. 'Now, it's been a tiring day, and everything will be a lot better in the morning. Why don't you snuggle down, and I'll stay here until you fall asleep. If you wake up, you can just call me, and I'll be in Granny's bedroom. OK?'

Talli nodded, and allowed Jenna to tuck her up. Jenna could see the girl glancing at the photographs on the dressing table opposite, one of Jake with Talli quite recently, and another older one of her mother with her as a toddler. Jenna's heart went out to her — it was rough to lose a mother so young. No wonder the child feared that Ailsa might die and leave her too.

Talli left her hand in Jenna's once the light was out, and the room was only illuminated by the glow of the night light. Sensing the tension in the child,

Jenna began to sing softly. All that came into her mind was one of the new songs she was writing, about Arasay and its landscape, the sea, the wind, and the mists. It was a gentle song, softly rocking in rhythm. At the end of the first chorus, a sleepy voice emanated from the bed. 'That's a nice song.'

Jenna smiled. 'Good.' She continued singing quietly. Gradually Talli's breath slowed, and after a while she slept. Jenna slipped her hand out of the small one, now limp, and crept from the room, leaving the door ajar so that she would hear if she called during the night.

16

Luckily, Talli's emotional exhaustion meant that she slept until morning, though Jenna's rest was more disturbed. Her mind was racing with ideas about how to entertain the child, what to say the next day to keep Talli happy. But when she finally got up at seven o'clock, knowing that she wouldn't sleep any more, she told herself firmly not to be a wimp. It was just practice, like everything else. All she could do was her best, be patient and kind and keep Talli occupied.

Jenna had just packed away their lunch dishes, while Talli was watching a video, when she heard the sound of a car drawing up outside. It was a large grey vehicle, which made her think it was the doctor again. Her heart began to pound, thinking that he was come to tell her something dreadful about Ailsa, and she hurried to the door.

However, on opening it, Jenna found an elegantly dressed older woman with short dark hair approaching. She was wearing beige narrow-cut trousers, and a camel-coloured casual jacket. She placed her feet in their caramel loafers carefully on the gravel path. The perfectly made-up face was marred by a frown of uncertainty when she came face-to-face with Jenna.

'Hello, honey, I'm looking for the Redman residence. I was told this was the right house.' The accent was clearly American.

Jenna glanced back indoors and saw that Talli had fallen asleep in front of the television. She stepped outside and closed the door softly behind her. 'You're at the right house, but I'm afraid that Mr Redman is away at the moment, and Mrs Redman is unwell.'

The frown deepened. 'Mrs Redman? Surely Jake's not remarried?'

'Mrs Redman is his mother. How may I help you?' Jenna felt a prickle of unease as she began to suspect the identity of the visitor.

'I've come to see my granddaughter. So who are you?'

Jenna's chest tightened as her fears were confirmed. So this was Gayle, Savannah's mother from America! What bad luck that both Jake and Ailsa were unavailable. How should she deal with this? She took a deep breath. 'I'm a family friend. My name's Jenna, and I'm looking after Talli for a few days until Ailsa's recovered.'

The woman's brow cleared. 'Well that's just great. I can take over from you, as her other grandmother. I'll tell my stepson to collect my suitcase from the hotel.'

Anger flared in Jenna. 'Now, just a minute! You can't just walk in here. Talli hasn't seen you since she was small, and I doubt she remembers you. I've been entrusted with her care and I won't let her be upset by a relative stranger. I can't let you see her without the permission of her father. I know he has been awarded sole custody.'

Jenna could see anger and confusion warring on the American woman's face, but then she shook her head and sighed. 'I don't know who you are or what your relationship is to my son-in-law, but you won't be hearing the last of this. I'm the child's grandmother and I have a right to see her. I haven't seen her for four years, and she's all I have left of my precious daughter.' Gayle's voice broke as she spoke these last words, and it tugged at Jenna's emotions as she began to see the situation from this woman's point of view and not just Jake's. But then she steeled herself. She didn't know the full story. Talli was her responsibility for the next few days, and she wasn't willing to go against Jake's wishes.

'I'm very sorry for your loss. I appreciate it was dreadful to lose your daughter, and that you've not seen your granddaughter for so long. But I can't go against the instructions of her father. He'll be home at the end of the week, and you'll be able to speak with him in person.' Jenna was aware of a male figure sitting in the driver's seat of the car, but couldn't see his face for the reflections on the windscreen. She hoped that her adversary wouldn't bring her stepson to her aid.

But the woman seemed to deflate. 'I can only spare these few days. I'm going home in two days' time as I have a business to run. Please, honey. Just let me say hello.'

Jenna shook her head. 'Talli's asleep.' But seeing the tears filling the older woman's eyes, she unbent a little. 'You can take a peek at her through the window — she's on the settee.'

Praying that the child wouldn't awaken, or that the woman wouldn't try to attract her attention, Jenna led her to the window. Conflicting emotions of pity and worry rippled through her as she saw the tears overflow on the woman's cheeks and heard a soft cry of anguish escape her tips.

'Oh my! She looks so like my

Savannah!' The woman instinctively put out a hand to the glass, but Jenna stopped her.

'Please — not now. That's all I can offer. I'll talk with Jake when he returns, and maybe he could telephone you and talk things through?'

Gayle took a handkerchief from her handbag and dabbed her cheeks. 'I suppose so. You must promise me that you'll put my case? I'm not the wicked grandmother he makes me out to be. I just love my baby girl and want to see her again, it's not too much to ask, is it?'

Jenna swallowed the lump in her throat and nodded. But her body was full of tension until they had driven off. What would she tell Jake?

Around half past four Jenna and Talli walked down to Ailsa's cottage to allow the child to spend some time with her. The older woman was still pale, but not as grey-looking as the day before. They only stayed for half an hour. Ailsa kissed Talli and said, 'Be good for Jenna.'

Talli was silent for a while on their walk, which disturbed Jenna, who thought that the visit would have reassured her. Then a thought struck her, and she stopped, taking the child's hand in hers. 'Talli, I don't want you to think of me as a teacher. Remember, I'm your daddy's special friend, which makes me a close person. More like an auntie.'

Talli looked at her quizzically. 'Have I to call you Jenna, like Daddy and Granny?'

She laughed. 'Well, I certainly don't want to be Miss Davidson! How about Auntie Jenna? That's means we're more than just friends.'

After what seemed a long silence, Talli gave a slow smile. 'I'd like that. I don't have any real aunties. I'd like you to be Auntie Jenna.'

The air cleared, they walked the last few metres to the house with lighter steps.

The telephone rang at six o'clock when Jenna was packing the dishwasher. She was pre-empted by Talli, who ran to the telephone. By the time Jenna entered the living room, the little girl was curled up on the settee speaking into the receiver. She looked up at Jenna with joy in her face, at the same time telling the caller that Auntie Jenna was looking after her because Granny was poorly. Relief flooded Jenna as she realised that it was Jake. Though at the same time she felt a pang of apprehension at how he would react to her living in his house for a few days.

After a few minutes, Talli passed the phone to her, saying that Daddy had asked to speak to her. 'But you've to hand the phone back to me so that he can say goodnight to me.'

Nodding, Jenna took the receiver. Jake was concerned, wanting the details of the crisis, which she explained. 'So I was really the only person available — I hope you don't mind.'

'Mind? Of course not! I'm grateful that you were able to step into the breach. It's at times like this that I wish I was just a writer or a carpenter, and I could work from home and be there for Talli.'

'But wildlife is your passion. You'd shrivel without it.'

He sighed. 'You're right. But it can be hard, being torn in two directions. How's my mother? Talli said you'd seen her for a while earlier.'

'She's still rather fragile, but Ian's keeping an eye on her. I think it'll be a day or two before she shows real improvement.' Her mind was crowded with the American grandmother's visit, but she knew that Jake had enough to take in without mentioning that.

'Unfortunately we're working in the mountains, so I won't be able to get a signal.'

Jenna assured him that all was in hand. Jake thanked her again, and promised to be in touch as soon as he was able. Jenna passed the phone back to Talli and went back into the kitchen. She chewed her fingernails, wondering whether she should have mentioned Gayle's visit, but judged this wasn't the time. With relief she looked up to find a happier child coming to draw her back into the living room.

The next day a dark blue car drew up outside the house, and Jenna's heart thumped with anxiety until a grey-haired man with a beard appeared at the door. He introduced himself as Peter Barr, Ailsa's neighbour and friend. 'I'm on my way into Balloch for some shopping for myself and for Ailsa. She gave me a list for you as well. Do you want to come?'

Talli was keen to go, so Jenna agreed. Their companion told them a little about himself as he drove the short distance into the village. 'I live half a mile inland from here, further down the track from Ailsa's cottage. I've been on Arasay for nine years — I write children's books about a family on a farm — I used to be a vet, myself.'

'I've seen your books on Talli's shelves.'

'Yes, I gave them to her. She likes my stories, don't you, Talli?'

Talli agreed. 'The one where Jack and his dog found the treasure in the caves was the best one. Chip the sheepdog is my favourite character.'

Once they reached the supermarket, Peter left them with their list while he shopped for himself and Ailsa. He then stowed all their bags in the boot of the car. Suddenly, Talli called out, 'Look, there's MacTavish! Can I go over to say hello, Auntie Jenna?'

Jenna looked up to see the small black and white terrier that had been Talli's playmate at Gobhar Castle. He was tied up by his lead to a bicycle stand at one side of the main supermarket entrance. Glancing round, she couldn't see any sign of Grant Fenton, so she allowed her to pet the dog. Jenna left her for a minute while she returned the trolley.

It was then she spied the dog's owner standing beside a Land Rover near the exit. He was talking with a large man, both gesturing as if they were arguing. Something about the other man stirred a memory in her, but she hadn't time to think about that now, not wanting Fenton to notice her. She called to the ecstatic child and cut short her reunion with MacTavish. 'We can't keep Peter waiting. We have to go.'

Reluctantly, Talli gave MacTavish one last hug and relinquished him. She gazed wistfully at the animal through the car window. 'MacTavish is really lovely. I wish I had a dog of my own.'

As they drove nearer the two men, Jenna had to swallow an exclamation as she recognised the large man — he was the American who had been so rude to her in the bookshop a few months ago. Was there any connection with Gayle's visit?

On the next two days, Ailsa came over for a couple of hours to mind Talli while Jenna was working at the bookshop, but it was tiring for her and she was happy to let Jenna take over when she was finished. Luckily Gayle didn't appear again. By Friday morning the older woman was well enough to resume her role. When she was waving Jenna off at the door, she thanked her sincerely for helping her out.

'I've enjoyed myself.' Jenna put her arms in the straps of her rucksack. 'I just hope that Talli hasn't been too disturbed by having me here.'

'It was different for her, that's true, but I think it was good that you had time to get to know each other properly. I don't know how your relationship with my son will turn out, or even if you want it to go further, but I won't stand in your way.'

Jenna's cheeks felt warm, hearing Ailsa talk so calmly about a possible future for her with Jake. She didn't quite know how to reply, as she and Jake had never discussed how serious they were. 'Well, no matter what happens, these few days have been lovely. Hope to see you again soon.'

Back in her room at Morag's house that evening, her phone began to buzz. Expecting it to be Jake, she glanced at the screen and was surprised to see that it was her mother. She told her about her time looking after Talli.

'I'm glad it went well,' Shona commented. 'Is Jake coming home soon?'

'He'll be home on Saturday.'

'Good — I hope we'll get a chance to meet him, your attractive cameraman.'

Jenna nearly dropped her phone. 'What do you mean? Are you coming to Arasay?'

'I thought it was time we visited you, as your dad and I are on holiday. Morag has kindly agreed to let us stay at her house. I hope you don't mind.'

Jenna sat down on the bed. Were her parents coming to give Jake the once over? Then happiness enveloped her, as she realised how much she'd missed them. 'Of course not, it'll be lovely to see you. When are you arriving?'

'Tomorrow, and we're staying until next Thursday. It'll be wonderful to see the island again, and to spend time with my lovely daughter.'

Jenna felt doubly excited at the

thought of her parents' arrival, coupled with Jakob's return. She hoped fervently that they would get on. She surmised that they might both be on the same ferry, but on the morning of their arrival, she received a call from Jake to say that he was home with Talli. He'd managed to get away a day early.

'How is Talli, and your mother?'

'They're both fine, but I know that my mother was relieved to get home to Peter.'

'To Peter? What did I miss?'

He laughed. 'They don't spread it about, and they live in their own homes, but they've been a couple for a few years now. It was a surprise to me when I first found out, but I'm glad that she has someone special in her life.'

His voice softened. 'Jenna, I'm so grateful for what you did. Plus I'm glad you and my family are getting on so well. It means a lot to me.'

Touched by his words, Jenna had to break the happy mood. 'Jake, something else happened while you were away.

Talli's American grandmother called at the house while I was there.'

'What?' His exclamation nearly deafened her. 'Did she see Talli — did you let her in?'

Jenna assured him that she hadn't. 'I knew you didn't want them to meet. Luckily Talli had nodded off on the settee in front of a video, and didn't realise that she was there.'

Jake became calmer. 'I'll need to get in touch with my solicitor. Is she still on Arasay?'

'I don't think so — she said she had to get back to her business. Jake — I let her look at Talli through the window. I must admit, I felt sorry for her. She lost her daughter, and hasn't seen her granddaughter for years. But I respected your wishes and didn't let them meet.'

There was a short silence on the other end of the phone, and Jenna's heart sank. Was Jake angry with her?

Finally he said, 'Did you tell my mother?'

'No, I didn't want to worry her while

she was ill. I believed Gayle when she said she was leaving.'

He gave a long sigh. 'Well, it looks as if we've escaped for just now, but we're going to have to be more vigilant from now on.'

'I'm sorry if I overstepped the mark.'

His voice brightened. 'No, you did right. It was just as well she didn't know you, as you were a good barrier. I understand you were moved — it's not so much Gayle as her stepson Warren who's the problem. I'm convinced that he led Savannah into a dark culture, probably even drugs. I suspect she may have been high when she crashed the car. I think Gayle paid to have the post mortem results doctored.'

'Jake, I'm so sorry. How awful for you.'

'Well, I'm glad you were able to protect Talli. I'll tell my mother what happened, and I'll get Andy McCrinan to check that she's left Arasay.'

'Are you coming to the ceilidh?'

'Unfortunately, no.' His voice was full

of regret. 'I think Talli needs to stay at home with me tonight, she's so thrilled to have me here.'

'One more thing — my parents are arriving on this afternoon's ferry to stay for a few days. How would you feel about meeting them some time?'

He mulled it over. 'Why don't we all meet up on Tuesday morning at the hotel at Uige on the north of the island? It's open to non-residents for coffee, and the lounge has wonderful views.'

'That sounds ideal.' A small stab of disappointment caught her at not being able to see him for three more days, but she understood that he wasn't a free agent, as she was.

It was wonderful to see her parents after their months of separation. Although she was loving her new life on Arasay, Jenna realised she had missed her family.

After attending the ceilidh on Saturday evening, Shona hugged Jenna. 'I can see that it's bringing you fulfilment.

What do the other members of the band think about playing with a former rock star?'

'I haven't told them — in fact, I haven't told anyone. I'm enjoying that I'm accepted for who I am, with no pre-conceived ideas.'

Shona frowned at this revelation. 'Have you told Jake?'

'Not yet — I haven't found the right time.' She bit her lip. 'It's only really in the past few weeks that we've been getting in deeper. I know I have to explain it all soon, but I'd be grateful if you both didn't say anything while you're here.'

Shona agreed, though she warned that it would be better to have things out in the open.

Jenna's parents spent the next few days reacquainting themselves with Arasay, and when Jenna wasn't busy at the bookshop, she joined them in their excursions. It was good to just be herself, loved unconditionally, with no expectations. Morag also flowered.

241

'I've missed having my family around me,' she told them.

On the Monday afternoon, Morag and Jenna were working in the book-shop, and Jenna was putting some new books on the shelves when she felt a strong hand on her shoulder.

'I wonder if you would mind showing me something in the back room?' Jake's deep voice spoke in her ear.

Jenna jumped up and took his hand in delight, pulling him into the stock room. Morag was busy at the till, so there was no-one to witness their reunion. Drawing her into his arms, they kissed with eagerness, the sensation of his body against her own giving her a delicious thrill. Then Jenna pulled back, and touched his face. 'The beard's quite full. I'm not sure how I feel about that.'

Laughing, he brushed his chin against her forehead, at which she giggled. 'I think you're turning into one of your subjects. A bear?'

He growled playfully into her neck,

which caused her to emit an exclamation, which she immediately stifled. 'We'd better be more circumspect. I don't want to shock Morag.' He hugged her close. 'I'll shave off the beard if you think it'll discourage your parents.'

She shook her head. 'No, that's fine. Or maybe just trim it a bit. I rather like it.'

Then Jake became serious. 'I've checked with Andy. Gayle and Warren have definitely left the island. They went the day after you saw them.'

Jenna searched his face. 'What are you going to do?'

'I've told my solicitor, and he'll make contact, telling Gayle to stay away.'

'She seemed to be genuinely upset and missing Talli.'

He ran his hand over his beard. 'Maybe she is. But will she respect my custody? I'm afraid if I leave her alone with Talli, she'd take her away and I'd never see her again.'

The anguish in his voice cut through to Jenna's heart, and she put her arms round him. 'You must do what you feel is right, but she did ask to speak with you.'

He closed his eyes for a moment, then said, 'I've got to go, though I wish I could stay longer.' He kissed her tenderly on the lips. 'Thanks for what you did to protect Talli.'

After they parted, Jenna returned to her work with a warm glow inside her. Clearly he hadn't just wanted to talk over Gayle's visit, he'd wanted to see her as well.

The following morning, Jenna's father drove them to the beautiful Uige Hotel. Only ten years old, its sweeping white curves imitated the undulations of the surrounding landscape. They found Jake in the gardens with Talli, who ran excitedly to Jenna, seemingly unfazed by the fact that she was accompanied by two strangers. Jenna made the introductions. Talli showed off her new toy, a cuddly snow leopard.

'I think it's the most beautiful of all my animals. When I'm older I'm going to photograph real ones, like Daddy.'

Her enthusiasm buoyed them all as they made their way towards the lounge. Having her there dispelled any stiffness from their meeting and made it pleasingly relaxed. Whenever Jenna's eyes met Jake's, he smiled at her tenderly, and at one point she caught her mother observing them, and Shona winked at her daughter. They stayed for a couple of hours, then headed off to their respective homes.

'I think you've found a good one there,' her father commented as he drove out of the car park behind Jake's Land Rover.

'Jake's obviously a caring man,' Shona agreed. 'Strange to think of him living in my old home. It was nice of him to offer to show us round, but I think I'll leave that until our next visit.'

Before her parents left the island, Shona said quietly, 'I know you're getting in deep with Jake, but before you commit yourself to anything, just consider his lifestyle. He's away an awful lot. Is he just looking for someone to be a mother to his child, and make his life easier?'

Jenna denied this strongly, but there was a hollow within her as she waved them off for the ferry. It had been wonderful seeing them again, and reassuring that they had got on well with Jake and Talli. But had it just stirred up doubts that she had not wanted to consider herself?

17

A week later, in mid-August, the children started back at school. Jenna had a week's grace before her teaching began once more, which was just as well because the island was still busy with holidaymakers until the English school term commenced at the beginning of September. Jake was to be working at home with only a couple of three-day stints in Glasgow until the middle of October, when he was due to be away for almost a month filming in Africa.

At the start of September, Morag discussed the bookshop with Jenna. 'I feel it's time for me to cut down, as I'm going to have my sixty-fifth birthday in January. We only open on two afternoons a week in winter, so how would you feel about taking over as manager of the bookshop? You don't need to commit fully yet, just make it a trial.'

Astonished, Jenna laid down the bundle of cards she was loading on to the racks. 'Are you sure you want to pass the job over to me?'

Morag waved away her thanks. 'You've taken to it very well. Obviously I won't be able to pay you as much in winter, but it's good that you've found other sources of income, with your music. Hopefully you'll get regular royalties from your songs as well.'

Jenna looked round to make sure the two customers currently in the bookshop were out of earshot. 'That remains to be seen. I heard from my solicitor yesterday that the hearing is set for October, in London. I'll need to take a week off.'

Morag straightened up a line of books on the shelf behind the main counter. 'No problem. I can call in Caitlin if I need help, and it'll be winter hours.' She turned to face Jenna. 'Are you still keen on moving into a place of your own? Some friends at the choir have a one-bedroomed chalet available from the second week in September.'

Jenna's face brightened. 'Is it nearby, as I'll need to cycle to Balloch and also to the school?'

Morag unfolded a map of Arasay and pointed to the location of the accommodation. 'It's between Balloch and Jake's house, so you'll have the best of both worlds. It's a little further to the school, but that's only one morning a week, isn't it?'

Excitement welled up inside Jenna. 'The position looks ideal. I wonder if I'll be able to afford it?'

'I'll give you the telephone number of the owners and you can arrange to view. You should be able to negotiate lower rent for a long let.'

Jenna hugged Morag in gratitude. She looked over the accommodation that weekend on changeover day before the final visitors came in. The owners were a couple whose children had left home in the past few years, and they had several properties on their land.

Jenna was delighted to find that it was a free-standing wood cabin just eight years old, overlooking the loch at Balloch.

Taking a liking to Fiona and Doug, Jenna was able to agree an affordable rent, and arranged to move in ten days later. The evening before she left, she cooked a special meal with Morag, after which they sat with glasses of wine, looking over the old family albums and reminiscing about Jenna's childhood visits, and all that had happened since she'd returned to Arasay.

Her aunt emptied out the last of the wine bottle into their glasses. 'I can't thank you enough for coming to my aid after my accident. I felt so helpless and such a drag on everyone, but having your company has been a joy to me. And to know that one of my family has chosen to live on the island is wonderful.'

There was a lump in Jenna's throat at Morag's words. 'It came at the right time for me — I had lost my direction, so helping you gave me a purpose. I've grown to love the island so much.'

'Of course, there has been an added incentive, with a certain good-looking photographer and his family.' Morag's eyes twinkled.

Jenna blushed. 'I never imagined that I would meet someone who would become so special to me. I keep telling myself that I mustn't surrender too deeply until his motives are clear — and my own, for that matter.' She became serious. 'Mum thought that Jake might be looking for someone to look after his daughter.'

Morag laid down her glass and reached out to put a hand on Jenna's arm. 'Jenna, he won't rush into anything if he doesn't think you're the right person for him. After all, Kezia's been close to the family since she returned to the island, too, and she never became any more than the mother of his daughter's friend, no matter how much more she wanted. I'm certain that Jake is interested in a future with you, but these things take time to develop. And of course he wants a mother for his daughter — that's part of the package. I don't think that's a problem for you, either.'

'No, you're right. I just want to be sure that I make the right choices. Plus I've never found the right moment to tell him about my past. I must be courageous and do it soon.'

The next morning, Jake brought the Land Rover to load it up with Jenna's stuff. 'I've ordered my new piano online, and it's coming next week!' she said as they drove towards her new abode.

'I look forward to you serenading me in the comfort of your own home,' he grinned. Once he'd halted the vehicle outside the cabin, it didn't take long to unload her belongings, along with a box of groceries that they had collected en route. After sharing a coffee, Jake left to let her unpack and settle in. He was due to leave on one of his three-day excursions to Glasgow to do some voice-over work for a previous project.

She had loved having him to herself in her own place, no matter how brief the moment had been. Laughing together and talking over their plans for the coming weeks had felt so right.

The band had a session on the Friday evening. They were now including Jenna's new song about Arasay, *Island of Mists*. Ruaridh had heard her tinkering with it one day before the band rehearsal, and had asked if he could try singing it.

'It's in English, not Gaelic,' she'd said apologetically. 'I love the sounds of the Gaelic language, but you need to be a fluent speaker to write words.'

'Well, Rabbie Burns also wrote in English, so that's no problem,' he'd replied, leaning over her shoulder to hum the melody. 'Jenna, that's such a great song. You have real talent.'

Jenna knew that composing songs was one of her strengths, but having written in a different style for so long, she couldn't be sure if there was any merit in these new songs from her heart. It boosted her confidence to hear Ruaridh's appreciation. Once he began to sing in his own inimitable style, she began to understand what he had heard in the song, and to see its potential. She resisted the urge to add her own vocal harmony, as it might be reminiscent of Urban Hawk. The rest of the band were happy to join in.

After the session, they repaired to the bar where drinks were waiting for them. A couple from Ireland were sitting at a nearby table, and the man stood up and came to chat with them. 'Do you have a CD, or a download site?' he asked.

Yet again, they had to give a negative reply. Craig took a sip from his beer, deep in thought, after the man had returned to his table. 'More and more people are asking us about a recording. We could be missing out on an extra source of income. I wonder how much it would cost to get a CD made for the next season?'

'We'd need a website too,' Ruaridh added.

Hamish laid down his glass. 'I could do that — but I've no idea about the recording.'

Jenna took a deep breath. 'I know something about it, through my old job. We could hire a recording studio in Glasgow for a day with an engineer.'

Ruaridh's face lit up. 'That's great! I say that we should go for it! What sort of price do they talk about?'

'There's one that I know is good and not too expensive.' She named a price that she thought was roughly the right amount.

Craig looked at the other two men, and seeing their nod of agreement, asked, 'How long ahead would we need to book?'

Jenna agreed to make enquiries, and the rest of their evening was spent discussing what tracks to include on the CD.

'And of course, we need to include Jenna's song about Arasay — that could be our signature tune, as the Arasay band.' Ruaridh added.

The other two agreed, which filled her with happiness. Her creative powers at last had a new outlet.

18

Ruaridh delivered her new digital piano the following Tuesday. Jenna was buzzing with excitement as she set it up. The bookshop was only opening on Wednesday and Saturday afternoons, so it meant that she could spend that afternoon exploring her new instrument, and making music to her heart's content. She even began a new song, and it occurred to her that she might actually compose a whole album herself. Could this be the way forward for her creativity?

Jenna and Jake crammed in as much time together as they could, as October was fast approaching and he would be off to Africa for his latest assignment. He took her on a couple of photographic excursions. The first was to watch the fallow deer which were in the rutting season, where she was amazed to witness a tussle between two stags competing for females. The second was a quieter day observing red squirrels in the woods round Arasay House, scurrying up and down trees and burying nuts for their winter stores. He offered her the use of his computer and printer to produce copies of their favourite shots to hang on the walls of her new home.

Jenna had booked the recording session in Glasgow for the beginning of October. Ruaridh drove them all in one of his SUVs. Rachel wasn't playing on all the tracks, but they had decided that the bodhran would add interest to some tunes. They hoped that it wouldn't just be tourists who bought the recording, and that it might get some wider recognition.

'There's a lot of competition,' Ruaridh commented wryly as they mounted the steps to the studio. 'There are so many professional bands on the go, and also lots of small local outfits like ours, so I suppose it's a bit of a gamble as to whether we ever make any money out of it.'

'Well, it might take a few years, but once we've got the master, we can get more CDs pressed whenever we need them. We can set up downloads online too. It's an investment for the future.' Jenna pressed the buzzer on the entry intercom to announce their arrival.

It was an exciting but exhausting day. Jenna was familiar with the environment, having recorded four albums with Urban Hawk so she felt some responsibility for the other members of the Arasay band, and that made her a little tense. Thankfully, once they were under way, everyone began to enjoy themselves, and they played well. The excitement of the occasion gave their performances an edge that they had never had before. Listening back on headphones to the recorded music in the studio, Jenna was thrilled to see the wonder of the other band members as they heard themselves for the first time.

At the end of the session, they

thanked the recording staff and packed up their instruments to leave. As they quitted the studio, one of the engineers came up to Jenna, smiling. 'So that's where you've been hiding, Linnet. Is this your new music? That song of yours, are you going to do a whole album? I hope you keep us in mind when you're ready to record.'

Jenna felt as if she'd been punched in the gut. With a gasp, she stammered, 'No, I'm not recording anything else, just the band today.' Then she regained her composure. 'I'd appreciate it if you didn't say that you'd seen me. I'm going under the name of Jenna Davidson now. If you keep that confidential, I'll let you know when I'm ready to do some more recording.' She looked the engineer boldly in the eye.

He returned her stare, then nodded, understanding. 'OK, that's fine by me. Good to see you again, Linnet — I mean, Jenna.'

The rest of the band were waiting for her outside. They stared at her with one accord, their faces blank with shock. 'Is it true?' Craig was first to say. 'Are you really Linnet, from Urban Hawk?' His brows were drawn together accusingly.

Jenna was dismayed at his expression. 'I was Linnet, but I've left Urban Hawk, and I've chosen to make a new life on Arasay.'

'Why didn't you say anything?' Ruaridh's brow was creased. 'Didn't you trust us?'

Jenna threw up a hand. 'I'm sorry, I truly am. I wasn't trying to deceive anyone. I just wanted to get away from my old life.'

'Well, it seems to me that you've been using us. Condescending to play with a cosy little ceilidh band to keep your hand in.' Craig's expression was accusing. 'Come on guys, let's leave her to her music buddies. We'll discuss this and let you know what we want to do about the recording.' He dug his fingers into Ruaridh's shoulder, pulling him round, and picked up his accordion case with his other arm. Hamish gave

Jenna a sheepish glance and followed the other men.

Ruaridh turned his head briefly, muttering 'Sorry,' as they walked away. Rachel remained where she was, her head on one side. Her demeanour was curious rather than accusing.

'Let's get a taxi back to the hotel, and we can have a talk. I want to know the whole story. I know you're a decent person, and you wouldn't treat people badly.'

Once they had reached their shared room, Rachel laid down her bodhran case and took off her coat and scarf. Without a further word, she went over to the minibar fridge and removed a couple of miniatures. 'Vodka or whisky?'

Jenna took the tiny vodka bottle. The two women sat opposite each other on their beds. Once she had downed a mouthful of the spirit and felt it burning her throat, Jenna faced Rachel and took a deep ragged breath. 'When I came to Arasay, I really was just coming to help Aunt Morag, and to recuperate after my bout of pneumonia. I wanted to leave Hawk, and to live in a place where I wasn't judged by who I had been. You've no idea what expectations that gives people.' She took a sip of her drink, then cradled the little bottle in her hands, which were trembling slightly. 'Plus I didn't want the media following me. It would have ruined any hope of a normal life here for me.

'I was only planning to stay for a couple of months. I never expected to find a new life here — music, friends, open spaces where I could breathe again.'

'And love?' Rachel added softly.

Jenna's eyes flew open. 'And love,' she echoed softly. 'I'm so enjoying being with Jake, and growing to know Talli.'

'Does he know — about your past?'

Jenna sighed. 'No. I've been telling myself for weeks now that I need to confess to him, but the time never seemed to be right. Now I expect he'll feel that I've been deceitful.'

'But you'll open up when you next see him?'

'Of course. Oh, Rachel, I've made such a mess of things!' She drained the last of her drink. 'But I did so want to live as myself, and not be judged by my public image.'

Rachel leaned across and laid a hand on her arm. 'Just be honest with Jake. I can see that you love the island, and you're not playing with us. Anyone who listens to your song can hear that. Craig just lashed out with the shock.'

Jenna nodded, wiping the corner of her eye. Rachel gave her a hug.

'I think we should find a movie on the TV, and get in a bottle of wine. We've had a long day.'

Jenna acknowledged that this was a good idea, and they managed to find something to watch that was congenial to both of them — though in the end she didn't drink very much of the wine. After a restless night, Rachel phoned Ruaridh, to check that he'd be willing to take Jenna back with them. It was a strained journey. Though Rachel tried to make some conversation, the men only replied in monosyllables, and there were long silences. Jenna found her head nodding frequently because of fatigue and lack of sleep. On the ferry, the men went to the bar while Rachel and Jenna sat in the lounge. It was too windy and wet to sit outside.

They dropped Jenna off at her new place. When she closed the door behind her, she allowed herself a session of misery and worry, then shook herself and began sorting out a load of washing. It was Friday, and Jake would be home again on Sunday. She would have the bookshop tomorrow, but there was no ceilidh as they were into the winter schedule, and October's had been last weekend. It would be three more weeks before the next one. But she decided to stay out of the way until the band had made up their minds about what they wanted of her. A brief sensation of panic arced through her as she emptied the washing machine, wondering what she would do if they ostracised her. Would it be enough to just work in the bookshop, teach her pupils at the school and write her own songs at home?

Jenna was waiting from a call from Jake on the Sunday evening to tell her that he was home. He'd been due on the lunchtime ferry, but so far there had been no communication from him. Finally she gave in and sent him a text.

Are you home yet? Is everything OK?

After a few minutes a reply came. *Some stuff to sort out. I'll check in later.*

Her solar plexus knotted as she read the terse words. What did he mean? In the end she gave up pacing around and began to play the piano, but couldn't concentrate. Instead she picked up the TV remote to flick through channels. She settled on a historical drama, though her mind wouldn't focus on what was happening in the story.

Just before half past nine, she heard

the sound of wheels on the gravel. Jumping to her feet, she saw the sweep of headlights as a vehicle swung into the parking place opposite. At last! A figure got out and strode towards her door, but she had opened it before he arrived.

The smile on her face died the moment she saw his expression. It was stony, dull. 'I can't stay long,' he said as he stepped inside. Jenna felt as if she had been slapped. She took a pace back and put her hand on her piano, feeling the solidity of its hard surface under her fingers.

Jake didn't make any move to follow her, but stayed just inside the door. 'I received a strange phone call from Kezia, and I'd like to know if what she told me is true.'

'What do you mean? What did she say?'

'She said that Ruaridh had told her that you're actually Linnet, that girl from the pop group. The one who left the group in the lurch and vanished?'

Jenna gave a sigh of despair. 'Jake,

that's not what happened at all. Yes, I was Linnet. But I'm also Jenna Davidson, Morag Buchanan's great niece, and I came here to help her.'

'Why didn't you tell anyone who you really were?' His gaze was hard.

'Linnet isn't my real self! I was in Urban Hawk, yes, and I wrote most of their songs. But I ended up with burnout, because I was unhappy, and I became seriously ill. When I recovered I knew I didn't want to go back. Devon was plaguing me because he said they couldn't do without me, but once I refused, he swore to sue me for breach of contract. I have a court hearing next month.'

He folded his arms. 'So when were you going to tell me? I thought we had something special, but you couldn't even trust me enough to tell me the truth about your past. I'm assuming Devon is Niall, the man you had the relationship with.'

She nodded miserably. 'I was wrong to keep it from you, and I'm sorry. I'd been hiding for so long and I was scared someone would bring the media circus down on me. I just couldn't cope with that.' Her voice trembled.

'Jenna, you surely didn't believe that I would run to the newspapers with any story about you?' His eyes flashed with anger.

'Of course not! I was just trying to find the right time, and the right words . . . ' her voice trailed off when she realised that nothing she could say would appease him. Her heart felt as if it had snapped, and she gave a gasp of despair.

He was unmoving. 'I need to process this. I'm sorry, but I think it's best if we don't see each other for a while. I'm off to Africa next Thursday. When I come back in three weeks we can talk.'

'Oh, Jake!' Jenna wanted to plead with him to reconsider, but she realised that his mind was made up. Taking a deep breath, she said, 'OK, if that's what you want. But I hope you realise that the person who has been dating you these past few months is the real me, not that false image of the rock star Linnet. She's firmly in my past, now, but I'm going to fight Devon for the rights to my songs and my income. I love my life here, my teaching, the bookshop, and the band, although I don't know if they'll take me back now. I feel at home on Arasay, and I'm staying no matter what.' It was only when she said these words defiantly that she realised that they were true.

He paused for a few seconds before nodding. 'I'll be in touch when I get back.' The anger seemed to have gone from his face, but she couldn't read his expression any further. Through blurred vision she saw him exit and close the door gently behind him. She couldn't move as she heard the engine start up again, and saw the headlights move off down the track. Then she flung herself into a chair and let herself give way to tears of remorse and regret.

It was hard for her to go into the school for her teaching session that week. Her heart contracted with love when Talli came in for her lesson, but she felt stiff with apprehension, wondering how she would behave. To her surprise, the child was as open and friendly as usual, and chatted about Daddy showing her some of his photographs from the latest shoot. She and Rosa were focused during the lesson, which made Jenna think that Jake hadn't mentioned anything of their quarrel to his daughter. As Talli exited, she turned back and said, 'Are you coming round to see us before Daddy goes away again?'

Jenna felt a stab to her heart, but kept her expression pleasant. 'We'll see. Daddy has a lot to do.'

'Well, you can come around after he's gone.'

'Maybe.' Jenna was glad that the next pupils were waiting to enter, so she didn't have to prolong the conversation.

Rachel came over to her cottage that evening. She had borrowed her neighbour's car, which she explained was an arrangement they had decided upon some time ago. 'I'm on the insurance, and it means I don't have the outlay of my own car. I just pay a share of the expenses, according to how often I use it.'

It was good to confide in a friend about the situation with Jake. After Jenna had poured out all that had happened, she added, 'You don't need to tell me what a fool I've been. I should have told him — after all, I trust him.'

'But you didn't want him to think of you as a different person, I can see that.'

'You're right, but it's worse that he now knows who I am and thinks that I'm deceitful as well.' Jenna sighed. 'What's more, I've got my hearing coming up in a couple of weeks. I'm scared of showing my new self in public, and I have to attend the court. What am I going to do?'

Rachel laid down her coffee mug. 'Well, why don't you just go as Linnet?

What did you look like when you were in the band? I seem to remember something about scarlet hair?'

Jenna grimaced. 'I don't want to dye my hair again. I like being unobtrusive.'

'It'd be easy enough to get a wig on the internet. Come on, let's go online and look!'

Within the hour they had ordered a scarlet curly wig in natural hair. 'I don't care about the expense, if it'll keep my identity safe for now. I just hope that none of the ceilidh band are on to a quick buck by selling the story to the media.' Jenna looked up at Rachel. 'For that matter, how did Kezia find out about it?'

'Don't you know? She and Ruaridh have been a couple for the past two months. Apparently he had a thing for her when they were at school.'

Jenna shook her head. 'So that's why she's not been making a fuss about me and Jake. But she obviously still has an agenda, if she told him about my past.'

'No, I don't think so. They're still

friends, and I believe she just thought that Jake should know.'

Jenna put her head in her hands. 'She was right — you're all right. My family have been saying for ages that I should open up. Why didn't I?'

Rachel squeezed her shoulder. 'Come on, it's not like you to be so negative. Jake's not said that it's over, just that he wants to think things through. You need to get your armour on and face the world. Concentrate on the hearing, and when that's over, rebuild your bridges. Hamish told me that Ruaridh is keen to get you back in the band.'

'Really? But Craig was so bitter about it.'

'Craig may be a bit harder, but I know that Hamish feels the same as Ruaridh.' The way that Rachel looked away and stroked a cushion self-consciously aroused Jenna's suspicions.

'So when did you get so chummy with Hamish?'

Rachel's cheeks looked pinker as she looked up with bright eyes. 'Well

274

— we've been seeing each other since last month. It was quite a surprise to me when he asked me for a date. After all, he's a couple of years younger than me.'

'That doesn't mean anything. Hamish is a great guy, and I'm so glad your love life is improving.' Jenna hugged her friend, pleased that she was finally putting her failed relationship behind her.

Rachel responded warmly. 'Now, don't worry about Craig. Let's see what happens when the CDs arrive. Let him stew for now.'

Jenna tried to do as her friend suggested. She flew to Glasgow for the mastering session for the CD the next day, and was told that their first copies should arrive within a couple of weeks. When she arrived back the following morning, she found that her mother had sent her black leather trousers and jacket from home, as requested. Tucked inside the parcel was her old makeup bag. Her fingers tensed as they closed round it. Time to make herself familiar again with the heavy black eye makeup and scarlet lips that had been her trademark look in Urban Hawk.

Scrutinising her made-up face in the mirror, it almost made her believe that the past year had been a dream, a fantasy interlude, and doubts began to overwhelm her once more. If she didn't have the band, and she didn't have Jake and his family, could she really stay on Arasay?

19

Later that week when Jenna was at the supermarket, she heard her name called. She straightened up to find Ailsa approaching her.

'I saw you when I was coming into the shop, and wondered if we could talk?' The older woman's demeanour was serious, causing Jenna some apprehension.

She nodded, and pushed her trolley to a quieter section away from the checkouts. It was raining heavily outside, and too cold to stand chatting.

Once they had halted, Ailsa continued quickly. 'Jake told me about your disagreement, and the reason why. No — don't say anything yet, let me finish. I want you to know that I can see why you kept your past quiet, and I don't hold that against you. Plus, I don't see why your previous career should affect anything about your relationship with my son. I know you want to leave all that behind you. I said as much to him, but he has a stubborn streak — he gets that from his father,' she added with an amused twitch of her lips.

Jenna felt herself becoming calmer, and thanked Ailsa. 'I hope he'll come to realise that I genuinely love it here on Arasay, and that this is the life I want. I just wanted him to know me as I am now. If only he would talk calmly with me.'

'Well, I hope he's having plenty of time to think while he's waiting about on location. Maybe it's just as well he's in a remote part of Africa. He'll have time to reflect on how happy he's been these past few months with you.'

Jenna felt herself blushing, astonished that Jake's mother should talk so frankly with her. 'I hope so too — I'm deeply involved with Jake, and with Talli too. I miss her as well.'

Ailsa put a hand on her arm. 'Well, we can remedy that. He never asked us to stay away from you, so why don't you come with us to the movie screening in the village hall tomorrow night? It's the new animation that everyone's raving about. Won't you join Talli and me for tea beforehand in the café? We could pick you up at four thirty.'

'I'd love to!' Jenna's mood soared.

It turned out to be a light-hearted evening, which soothed her raw emotions. Talli was so excited about the film that she could hardly eat her pizza. There were lots of other children at the picture. Kezia and Ruaridh were also there with Lachlan. They were sitting on the other side of the audience, but Ruaridh waved with a rueful smile. On the way out he called, 'I have a delivery for the bookshop. Would tomorrow morning around eleven be OK?'

Jenna agreed, realising that he wanted to talk in private before the shop opened. When he brought in the two boxes the next morning, she made them both a hot drink.

Ruaridh stared into the mug in his hands. 'I'm sorry I didn't back you up in Glasgow — I want you to know that it was just surprise that made me witless. I should have sussed it out sooner. After all, I have a couple of Urban Hawk albums, and I've seen videos on the internet. But you look totally different. People don't see things when they don't expect them. To think that Linnet was hiding out in plain sight all the time, playing in our humble band!' He looked up and grinned at her.

'Ruaridh, it's not a humble band! You're all fine musicians. Just because you don't play on the global scene doesn't mean you're any less good. In fact, you all have more genuine talent than a lot of people I've worked with in the past who make a professional music career. I've felt privileged to be a part of your band, and have enjoyed every minute of it. I hope you don't think I was using you to get back into the recording business.'

'Not at all. But it makes me see in a new light the fact you said you'd been writing a few songs. Are you intending doing a new solo album?'

As they discussed Jenna's new hopes and dreams for her music, she found that she was enjoying having such a frank talk with another musician. They agreed that when she had enough songs, she and Ruaridh would have a session together and he would perform on her new project if she so wished. 'I'm sure Hamish would be up for it as well, if you write in some fiddle. He's good at improvising, too.'

'But you don't think Craig would join in,' she said sadly.

'Craig's a hothead, but he'll come round.'

Just like someone else I know, she thought dismally. Would Jake ever accept her again?

The next two weeks flew past, and somehow the pain of losing Jake made her more productive in her song writing. Two new ones were polished and ready before she left for London for the hearing. Her black leathers, her makeup and the red wig were in her cabin bag for the plane. She flew from Arasay airport to Glasgow, then took a flight to London. She had booked into one of an unassuming chain of faceless hotels that wasn't too near the court.

After freshening up, she went to meet her parents, who were staying in another nearby hotel. They each folded her in a deep embrace. 'It's so good to see you,' she murmured.

Shona held her at arm's length and studied her face. 'How are you? Any word from Jake?'

Jenna had poured out the whole story of the quarrel over the telephone with her mother, and had been relieved that she hadn't said 'I told you so'. It was a balm to have her parents' unconditional love and support. 'No. But I don't want to talk about that now. Have you heard from Leo?' Her brother had told her that he would try and make it to the second day of the hearing, work permitting.

'He still thinks that he'll manage to get to the court on Wednesday,' Alan confirmed. 'He's in the television studio all day tomorrow, but should be finished by the end of the day.'

Jenna hugged them again. 'It means so much to me to have you here.'

'We couldn't let you face Devon on your own. I was surprised he turned out to be so vindictive. He always seemed a nice boy,' her mother said.

Jenna shook her head. 'Maybe he was, but he changed from that idealistic student. He was always a bit self-centred, but he became so focused on image and money, and that soured everything about the group for me.'

'Well, I hope he gets a kick in the teeth when we wipe the floor with him,' her father retorted.

Despite her anxiety, Jenna couldn't help giggling. 'Dad! That's a right old mix of expressions — and I didn't know you were such a fighter.'

Alan held her close with one arm.

'Anyone who threatens my little girl deserves that — and you can tell Jake that as well.'

'Thanks, Dad,' she said softly into his chest.

The next morning, Shona had arranged to meet Jenna at her solicitor's office. Jenna had brought her 'Linnet' outfit, and Shona helped her with the wig. After Jenna had applied her dark eye makeup and scarlet lips, she turned to her mother. 'Is that convincing enough?'

Shona nodded. 'I'd almost forgotten how you used to look. How does it feel?'

'Like a bad dream. I just want to get this over and get back to my own peaceful self on Arasay.'

Shona walked along the road to meet up with her husband in a café, while Jenna took a taxi with Kieron Warburton, the young solicitor who had briefed her in Glasgow earlier in the year. Richard Holman would be acting for her in court, and had gone separately so as not to draw attention to her. There was a flurry of media activity outside the court, with television cameras and reporters, but Kieron hurried her through, saying 'No comment' to all their shouted questions.

It was a stressful two days. She pretended not to notice Devon's glowering stare across the court room. A young woman sat by his side. Under his black waistcoat his chest was bare, showing several new tattoos, and he wore leather trousers. His hair was bleached and waxed, and he now had a tattoo sleeve. It was a far cry from the young man she had met at university all those years ago. Hearing his accusations about her laying claim to his ideas and leaving them in the lurch made her furious, but she kept her face impassive and allowed her legal team to do their job. She had little to say herself, as all the work of proof had been done in advance.

On the second day it was comforting to see Leo at the back of the spectators.

285

They had agreed not to make contact so that Jenna could become anonymous again after the hearing. By the end of the day she was ready to drop with weariness, but relief engulfed her at the verdict that the songs were judged to be eighty five percent her work (although she knew it was nearer one hundred percent) and she would still receive substantial royalties. Although she would have to pay damages for her breach of contract, the mitigating circumstances of her health meant that it wouldn't clean her out completely. There had been a clause in the contract about breakdown of health, which her solicitor had focused on. Her defence had pushed the fact that her lungs had been weakened by the pneumonia, and that she was unable to return to the band and their gruelling schedule of touring and live performances. She wouldn't have to pay costs as Devon had in effect lost his case.

Outside the court, she faced the cameras and microphones with calm confidence. She had prepared a short statement which her solicitor read out, declaring that she was pleased with the verdict, and she would appreciate being allowed to live her life quietly, out of the media spotlight. From the corner of her eye, she could see another posse of media surrounding Devon and his girlfriend. As she hurried to the car that Kieron had organised for her, she vowed that she wouldn't look at the internet for a long time, because she didn't want to read any more of Devon's lies and fabrications. Any feelings she'd had for him while they were together were totally dead, now, eclipsed by his treachery and the open, trusting love she had shared with Jake.

Jenna tried not to think about Jake as the car whisked her back to her solicitor's offices, and instead focused on her family. Her mother was waiting for her, and she helped Jenna remove her 'Linnet' wig and makeup. Back in her jeans and jumper, Jenna pulled on her black hooded jacket. They slipped out of the back way and walked a couple of blocks before hailing a black cab. Richard and Kieron had promised to keep the attention of any reporters who might have followed them while all this went on.

Back at her parents' hotel, her father and Leo were waiting in the lobby, and they all hugged her. 'You showed him!' Leo said, giving her a high five, which made her grin, despite her exhaustion.

'We've booked a table at a quiet restaurant that Leo knows not far from here, for eight o'clock. That'll give you time to gather yourself before eating,' her father told her.

Then she felt her mother squeeze her arm, but to her surprise she turned her round and pointed towards the door. 'I think there's someone else who wants to speak with you.'

Jenna's eyes widened. Her whole body trembled as she recognised the tall figure standing beside the door, advancing tentatively towards the family group. His hair was ruffled, his taut jaw lined with his short beard. 'Oh, Jake, why are you here?'

He nodded towards her parents and Leo. Shona pushed her daughter towards him, and the Davidsons melted back towards the bar area.

Jake stopped a couple of metres away from her. 'Jenna — I saw the verdict. I'm pleased that you've had a good result.' His voice was stilted and stiff. Then he added, 'Would you come outside for a few minutes, so we can talk? I know it's been a long day for you . . .'

Without waiting for him to finish, she took his hand and hurried outside into the night. They headed away from the extreme brightness of the windows at the front of the hotel, to a darker patch leading to the car park.

'I thought you were still in Africa,' was all she could say.

'I managed to get away a couple of days early. I wanted to see you — Jenna, I'm so sorry for all I said to you. I was thrown by what Kezia told me, and once I was away, I realised that she was passing on gossip, without your side of the story.'

'I was going to tell you. I just never found the right time. I wanted to move on from my past.'

'Do you feel that you can, now? I wish you'd told me what you were going through, with this hanging over your head.'

Tears filled Jenna's eyes. 'I was afraid that you would see me in a different light. I just wanted to be the woman in your life, not someone with fame behind them.'

He shook his head, a smile touching his lips. 'I was in court today, and saw you presenting such a brave face, listening to all that invective from Devon. You looked so serene, even in your Linnet gear, and I wanted to go and stand by your side, or even punch him on the nose!'

She laughed shakily. 'That would certainly have blown my cover!'

Without further words, he reached

out and pulled her into his arms. Jenna sank into the safety of his embrace, unable to prevent the tears running down her cheeks. For a few moments, he let her sob, stroking her hair, murmuring endearments to her. Then he kissed the top of her head. 'Jenna, once I was away from you I was so afraid that I'd lost you forever. I can't describe how happy you've made me over the past few months. I can honestly say that I've fallen deeply and truly in love with you, and can only ask if you might forgive me.'

She looked up at him, her eyes still shining with tears and with joy at the same time. 'Jake, I've been afraid to admit even to myself how much I love you. Plus I love Talli as well. I'm so grateful that you trust me with her.'

He then bent his head and kissed her lips tenderly. After a few moments they broke away.

Jenna stroked his arm. 'I think we'd better go back in to my family.'

Jake's arm was round her as they entered. Shona jumped to her feet, but the anxiety melted from her face when she saw them together. It turned out to be a comforting evening, though Jenna could hardly keep her eyes open at the restaurant, as her tension had ebbed away and the emotional energy had drained her. Jake had booked into the same hotel and took her back.

Next morning they headed off to their various destinations. Jake got a seat on Jenna's Glasgow flight, and also on the small plane to Arasay. They sat in silence for most of the journey, simply holding hands and enjoying each other's presence with the peace of those who know that they are secure in their love. Jenna smiled the whole way back home. It was a special moment when the little plane penetrated the cloud and Arasay came into view. Finally they approached the runway and touched down. Home! This was her future life, and happiness was overflowing from every part of her.

Jake had telephoned his mother before they left Glasgow, and once he and Jenna collected their luggage and walked through the airport they could see her car waiting. To their surprise, both Ailsa and Talli jumped out at their approach, the little girl still in her school uniform. She ran across to them and threw herself into Jake's arms. He swung her round and kissed her, laughing.

'Now, do you have a hug for Jenna, too?'

Jenna felt a momentary doubt at his words, but she needn't have worried, because Talli leaned over from her father's arms and let Jenna embrace her too. 'Hi, Auntie Jenna! I've been practising my recorder so that I'll be twice as good for next week's lesson!'

'Good for you!' she replied, releasing Talli back to Jake, who set her down and took her hand as they made the final steps towards the car. Ailsa was watching them with a serene smile on her face, and greeted them warmly.

Jenna felt that it was a perfect return to Arasay.

Next day she received a visit from Ruaridh. 'We've been talking, Hamish, Craig and I, and we want you to come back to the band. We had a rehearsal while you were away, and Craig admitted that he'd been a bit hasty. He's a good guy at heart, just a wee bit defensive when it comes to his musical abilities. He thought that maybe you were toying with us. But he's had time to think about it, and realised that you were always genuine about your enjoyment. He understood that you were in a difficult situation while the court case was pending.'

Jenna hugged him impulsively. 'Ruaridh, you've no idea how happy that makes me. I respect all of you — you're fine musicians, and I love working with you. As long as you don't mind the fact that I may release a solo album in my new style, under the name of Jenna Davidson. But it's going to be low key — I'm going to run the bookshop and teach at the school for the foreseeable future.'

He grinned. 'Fine by me. If you need any extra musicians for the album, let us know.'

'I'd love that.' Her eyes misted at the thought of making music again with these friends.

They met for a rehearsal that Friday evening, as they weren't playing regularly in the hotel during the winter months. Now Jenna was able to talk freely about all that had gone on at the court case, and answered their questions willingly.

When they retired to the bar of the hotel afterwards, Jake joined them, and it was a relaxed evening. It was almost eleven o'clock when they climbed into Jake's Land Rover, their warm breath soon misting the windscreen as they drove through the cold night. But to her surprise, he went straight past her cabin, towards the other side of the island.

'This is a special night,' he told her

when she questioned him. 'I've been keeping an eye on the weather reports, and we could be lucky.'

Looking up at the clear night sky dotted with stars, Jenna wondered what it could be. A comet — a meteor shower — a bright planet? It was approaching midnight when they finally stopped. Jake had some blankets in the back of the vehicle which he tucked around them. He produced a flask of hot tea, and poured them each a mug, which they sipped as the time went by.

Finally just after quarter past one, when Jenna's head was nodding on his shoulder, he shook her alert. 'Jenna, it's started. Look!'

Forcing her heavy eyelids open, Jenna peered through the windscreen at the sky. After a few moments she spied a strange green flicker towards the north. Gradually the ribbons of colour rippled more brightly, and realisation burst upon her. 'The Northern Lights! Jake, that's wonderful!'

Jake grabbed a camera and tripod,

and they stepped outside to have the best experience of the phenomenon. To their delight the green lights began to spread across the whole of the night sky, with flashes of gold interspersed. He took some photos, then they stood together, arms round each other, drinking in the spectacle.

'Thank you so much, Jake! I've dreamed of seeing the Aurora Borealis for years. This is absolutely magical.'

They kissed tenderly as nature performed its colourful dance above them. Then Jake looked deep into her eyes. 'Jenna, this is the perfect moment for what I have to ask you now. Jenna Linnet Davidson, will you marry me?'

With a gasp, she tried to take in his words, and finally was able to reply. 'Dear Jake, yes, I will.'

'There will be challenges. I'll still be away a lot, and you and Talli will be on your own — though of course my mother will be just down the road.'

Jenna felt a small sliver of anxiety. 'Do you think they'll be happy about me marrying you? After all, Talli has had you all to herself for such a long time, and your mother might feel that she's being usurped.'

He kissed away her fears. 'Don't worry, I put it to my daughter and she was delighted. She likes you, but in addition, thinks that this means she can get a dog, and maybe even a baby brother or sister!'

Jenna laughed. 'I suppose she might!' Then she added, 'What about your mother?'

'She's fine too. She said that she and Peter had been thinking of going on holiday together, and now she wouldn't be so tied. I assured her that we'll keep close.'

Jenna sighed and leaned her head on his chest, her doubts appeased.

20

The next afternoon, Jenna could hardly keep her mind on her work at the bookshop. She had phoned her family that morning, and they were delighted to hear of her engagement. Morag too was glowing at the exciting news. Jenna arranged for Kenneth, the Balloch taxi driver, to take her to Jake's home as soon as the bookshop closed. As they drove along the road, she marvelled at the wild waves crashing on to the shore, gilded by the moon, which was almost full.

'There's a fierce storm coming across the Atlantic,' Kenneth told her.

'This is my first experience of a storm on Arasay — I've heard they can be pretty bad.'

'Indeed.' Kenneth proceeded to tell her tales of power being cut off for days, and the ferry not reaching the island for a week or more in previous years. Jenna listened in fascination. The islanders were accustomed to the might of nature, and she was determined to embrace whatever it brought this time. The moon vanished and it began to rain before they reached Ballintroon.

Jenna was surprised to find Ailsa's car plus another one she didn't recognise parked outside the house. She wasn't expecting this to be a party — she'd thought it would just be Jake and Talli, welcoming her into the family unit. As she paid Kenneth, the door swung open and Jenna stifled a gasp when she recognised the figure of Gayle, the American grandmother, silhouetted in the doorway. Even more unexpected, she was hugging Talli. A tall unfamiliar figure in a waterproof black coat with a hood hurried past them and over to the large car parked beside Ailsa's. Jenna could hear Gayle calling, 'Bye, honey, see you tomorrow!' as she climbed into the car. She also waved to Jenna as the vehicle swept past the taxi.

Jenna made a dash for the house as a sheet of rain enveloped her. Jake was at the door, and kissed her quickly with a strange expression on his face before he ushered her inside. Talli skipped ahead of them into the living room, where Ailsa was shrugging herself into her waterproof coat.

The older woman's face brightened at her arrival, and she pulled her into a warm embrace, congratulating her and welcoming her to the family. 'I'll be off now and let you talk. We'll get together soon, I promise.'

Once she had left, Jake put his arm round his daughter. 'Talli, are you going to give Jenna a hug?'

Artlessly, the child skipped over to Jenna and threw her arms round her. 'Daddy says I can be bridesmaid when you get married. Can I wear a pink dress?'

Laughing, Jenna kissed the soft cheek and hugged her close. 'Of course! We'll choose it together once we've decided when the wedding will be.'

Inside the house, Jake explained that they were taking Talli to the Naylors' farm as it was her friend Rosa's birthday. 'They're due to have a sleepover.'

Talli chattered excitedly throughout the journey. Jenna understood that the arrival of the child's grandmother and the prospect of a new stepmother were two huge changes in her life. Once Jake had taken her into the farm and left her with the Naylor children and their mother, Zoe, he was able to talk freely about what had happened that afternoon.

He explained that Gayle had turned up unexpectedly, determined to talk with Jake and see Talli. His mouth was grim as he went on. 'I have to confess that I didn't tell you about the appeal of the custody hearing about six weeks ago, just before I went to Africa. That's one reason I was so grumpy with you, as it was preying on my mind, and I didn't want to discuss it with anyone. I'm sorry. Thankfully the judge ruled in my favour again.'

Jenna was quiet, feeling slightly disturbed that he hadn't felt able to confide in her. Then she shook herself. She couldn't complain, considering how she had kept so much from him. At least it was all in the open, now. 'Can she appeal again?'

'No, and thankfully she has less leverage now that you and I are engaged. We'll be a proper family unit, and she can't contest that. Talli will have a stepmother to look after her while I'm away.' His gaze was tender as he squeezed her hand.

Jenna relaxed, allowing her concerns to melt away. 'I'll do all I can to give her a mother's love. I think the world of Talli.'

'I know you do.' He reached for her hand and kissed it gently before continuing. 'Anyway, to return to Gayle, I didn't let her into the house until I'd called my mother and asked her to sit with Talli. Then I took Gayle and Warren — that's her stepson — down to my mother's cottage. I don't know why she has to always bring him with her as her driver. I can't stand the man.'

'So what happened?'

'We talked for about an hour and I must admit that I judged her feelings for Talli to be genuine. I let her come up to the house and be reunited with her.'

'Was Talli excited to see her grandmother again?'

'She was a bit wary at first, but she did remember her eventually. I knew you would be arriving, so I kept the meeting short. I said that Gayle could pick her up tomorrow lunchtime from the farm and spend a couple of hours with her on her own before she brings her back home.'

Jenna touched Jake's arm. 'That's a very generous gesture. I hope matters become easier now that you've made a truce.'

He sighed and turned into the entrance to Ballintroon. 'Well, I hope so. I'm still not entirely comfortable about it. I said it was too soon for Talli to go over to the States on her own to stay. Until she's older, I'd like Gayle to visit her here.'

They cooked a relaxing meal together, and began to make plans for their wedding, deciding that a date in May would be ideal. Afterwards, Jake took her to her cabin and kissed her lingeringly on her doorstep.

They arranged that Jenna would return to Ballintroon the following afternoon when Talli would be back home, so that they could begin to get to know each other as a family.

The next morning, the wind was wilder than ever. One of Jenna's windows faced the coast, and she could see that the sea was high. She and Rachel called off their Sunday morning cycle ride. Rain and wind accosted her cabin all day, and heavy dark clouds enveloped the island in gloom.

Jenna borrowed Fiona and Doug's car to drive to Ballintroon for five o'clock, because they weren't needing it. As she turned the windscreen wipers to their fastest speed, she mulled over what Gayle might think of her when Jake presented her as his future wife. Would she be resentful, seeing someone taking over the place of her daughter?

Only Jake's Land Rover was parked outside the house when she drew up. The door flung open at her approach, and Jake appeared, his face white and drawn, his hair standing on end as if he had run his hands through it many times.

'I thought it might be Gayle with Talli,' he gasped as he pulled her inside out of the lashing rain.

Pulling down her hood and wiping her wet face, Jenna looked at him quizzically. 'Where are they?'

'I'd love to know. Gayle was to pick Talli up from the Naylors' farm late morning and take her for lunch, so that they could have some time together.

They should have been here hours ago.'

'Could they still be at the farm?'

He shook his head. 'I phoned Zoe early afternoon, and she told me that Gayle had arrived at the appointed time, with Warren driving. Talli had been quite happy to get in the car with her grandmother, and the last Zoe saw of them they were heading off down the track to the road. That was six hours ago.'

'But where could they have gone?'

'I've already contacted the hotel, and they checked Gayle's and Warren's rooms. There was no one there, but their luggage was still in place. The ferry isn't running, and won't do for the next few days, so they haven't left.' He paced up and down, looking out of the window.

'Maybe they've just gone somewhere else and lost track of the time.'

'Jenna, it's pitch black out there! They're strangers who don't know the island, and the hazards of a single-track road. Why would they go off with her?' He grasped a fistful of his hair and tugged it at random.

She hugged him. 'Jake, have you contacted the police?' Something was nagging at her in the back of her mind, a hint of a memory that was disturbing, and she felt it was somehow connected to this situation.

'That's my next plan. Now that it's dark I know there's something seriously wrong.'

Suddenly her mind flashed into clarity as she recalled the previous day, when Gayle and her stepson had exited the door. She gasped, which made Jake swing round. 'Jake, I've just realised that I've seen Warren twice before. He was in the bookshop back in May, buying maps, and was quite rude to me. I thought him a distinctly unpleasant person. Then, when I was looking after Talli in the summer, I saw him in the car park of the supermarket talking with Grant Fenton, and he looked as if he knew him pretty well.'

'Fenton? Why didn't you tell me this before?'

'I'm sorry — I didn't know he was Gayle's stepson. I only caught a glimpse of him yesterday, though I felt a slight recognition that I couldn't place.'

'I'm getting on to Andy straight away. 'It only took ten minutes for the police vehicle to reach Ballintroon. Andy removed his cap and frowned as Jake elaborated on the situation.

'I'm concerned about Warren having connections with Fenton, who seems to have tried to become familiar with Talli through his dog.' Jake's expression was grim.

The policeman nodded. 'We've been keeping an eye on Grant Fenton — he's a known felon on the mainland. He doesn't seem to have put a foot wrong here so far, but he's wormed his way into lots of businesses with his odd jobs — the garage, the fish farm, and a bit of crab fishing as well.'

'I'm convinced he was driving that fish farm lorry that ran me down earlier in the summer,' Jenna exclaimed.

Andy gave a brief nod. 'I wouldn't be

surprised. Right, Jake, I'll get my deputy to search Fenton's home, and I'm going to visit a few other places round the island now that we have a connection.' He replaced his cap and went out of the door.

Jake grabbed a coat. 'I'm going out on the road myself. You stay here with my mother, Jenna, and I'll ring you if I strike lucky.'

'Please take me with you.' She grasped his arm. 'As long as I'm not in the way. But another pair of eyes could be helpful.'

He paused for an instant before pulling her close and sighing into her hair. 'OK.'

They were telling Ailsa of their plans, when all the lights suddenly went out.

'That's all we need — the power's down,' he grumbled.

Ailsa was on her feet. 'I'll get the generator going.'

Jenna looked at them both in bewilderment. They seemed quite accustomed to this.

Ailsa added, 'I've been charging the walkie-talkies. Here.' She handed him a small gadget about the size of a mobile phone. He switched it on, then kissed his mother on the cheek.

'We're vulnerable to power outages when there's a storm of this magnitude. Mobile signals could be useless. But these give us a better chance of staying in touch with each other.'

They took their waterproofs, a couple of blankets and some other tools and rope. 'We have no idea what happened to them — they could need a tow.'

Jenna followed his lead willingly. Jake's experience of the island and his work in wild places had given him valuable experience. The Land Rover was buffeted by the high wind, and the rain battering on the windscreen made it difficult to see in the dark. The headlights only served to illuminate the sheeting rain, and Jenna had no idea how he managed to instinctively drive the roads without ending up in a ditch.

Hour after hour they drove round. At

one point they met another vehicle, which turned out to be Andy McCrinan's. Both stopped and wound down their windows to shout questions at each other over the driving roar of the wind and rain. Jenna heard enough snatches of Andy's replies to know that his investigations had yielded nothing, and her spirits sank lower.

It was nearing midnight when Jake finished his circuit of the island back to Ballintroon, and he admitted that they should try and get some rest and begin searching again at daybreak. Ailsa was still waiting up for them, her face bleak. She knew that they would have tried to contact her had they found their quarry.

'I've put clean sheets on Jake's bed for you — he'll use the inflatable mattress down here.'

All of them only had fitful sleep. Jenna was disturbed by the roaring, of the wind and rain against the house, and her mind was filled with anxiety at the thought of a child out in this mayhem, with only two virtual strangers who were unfamiliar with the conditions. How Jake was feeling, she could only imagine.

Eventually she was aware of murmuring voices downstairs. Throwing her clothes back on, she went down to join Jake and Ailsa. They were eating bread and honey, and a kettle was about to boil on a small primus stove. Ailsa filled two flasks while Jenna ate some breakfast, forcing down the food to try and give herself some energy for the day ahead. The sky was beginning to lighten.

Jake spoke little, and Jenna felt as if she was in a waking nightmare. As they headed out to the Land Rover she queried, 'Is the storm passing yet?'

'It's abating a little. But the power may stay off for a few days until the services get it fixed.'

Once they were on the road again, Jake began to investigate tracks that led off to the hills, or to beaches. After a fruitless hour Jenna recognised that they were heading towards the islet with the causeway where he had taken her to look for otters all those months ago.

'This could be tricky — the tide's coming in, and it'll be worse in this weather,' he muttered as the causeway came into view, lashed by the encroaching sea.

'Look, Jake, there's a car — oh no, it looks as if it's crashed!'

The dark grey car was barely off the islet and on the causeway on the other side, facing them, but it was hanging down the side of the bank, the bonnet already partially submerged by the rising tide. Surging waves were breaking over the driver's side, where the door was open.

'The sea's higher than normal.' Then he gave an exclamation. 'There's someone hanging on to the driver's door — it's Gayle!'

'Can you see Talli?'

'I think there's a small figure in the passenger seat, which is higher on the causeway. It's about the right size for her.'

He gunned the Land Rover forward, but before he could advance more than a few metres, a huge wave engulfed the causeway. To their horror, they saw Gayle's car slip lower down the bank where it was almost completely submerged. The figure clinging to the door disappeared into the water. At the same time, about ten metres of causeway in front of Jake's Land Rover crumbled and disappeared into the boiling sea.

With a cry, Jake erupted from the vehicle, pausing only to shout, 'I'm taking the rope — tie the other end securely to the Rover. Then call my mother on the walkie-talkie and get her to send help.'

Without giving herself time to think, Jenna leaped out and took the end of the rope that he tossed to her, and attached it as firmly as she could to the bumper of the Land Rover, thankful that her father had taught her some strong sailing knots. Then she watched in trepidation as Jake waded into the water, and as soon as the ground disappeared under his feet, he began to swim, striking out determinedly towards the grey car.

With each gust of wind came a surge of water, sometimes breaking over his head. Jenna kept her eyes on him while she slipped back into the driver's seat of the Land Rover to use the walkie-talkie. 'Ailsa, it's Jenna, can you hear me?'

There were a few heart-stopping seconds of silence as Jenna continued to watch Jake fighting through the turbulent water.

A crackling reply broke the silence. 'Jenna, I can hear you! Have you found them?'

'Yes, but there's been an accident. The causeway to the Otter Island has been washed away, and their car is in a perilous situation. Jake's swimming out to get Talli. Gayle fell into the water and I can't see her.'

Ailsa cried out in dismay. 'I'll get on to the police at once. I wish I could be there to help. Let me know as soon as they're safe.'

Jenna agreed, and slipped the handset into the pocket of her waterproof. She gave a silent prayer as she saw Jake finally reach the car, and through the rivulets running down the windscreen she was thankful to witness him climb up on to what remained of the causeway. He reached into the grey car and loosened Talli from her seat belt, taking her into his arms and hugging her close. Then he waved to Jenna.

Surely he wasn't going to try and swim back with Talli? Jenna leaped from the vehicle, wondering if she could somehow help pull them across. Maybe she could reverse the Land Rover down the track. But if he didn't swim, how else would they get back?

At that moment she heard a motor engine behind her, and swung round to see Ruaridh's van approaching. He pulled up smartly and leaped out. An older man was with him.

Ruaridh took in the scene with one

glance, and waved to Jake. After a few hand gestures, he turned back to Jenna. 'The causeway is impassable. We've got to get them back quickly, otherwise Jake will become hypothermic, and the car will become submerged. I'll back the Land Rover down the path, and Dad can help you reel in the rope. That should work.'

Nodding frantically, Jenna went forward to grasp the rope, the older man picking it up behind her. She noticed him checking her knots and nodding, which gave her some satisfaction. Ruaridh shouted out of the window of the vehicle. 'Ready? Signal to Jake to get into the water.'

Jenna could see Talli clinging to her father's neck, her little face contorted with fear as he slipped into the waves. Once Ruaridh began backing down the track, they managed to winch the two across in record time. Within moments Ruaridh's father was pulling Jake and Talli out of the water, and Jenna was running to the Land Rover to grab blankets and towels.

'I couldn't see Gayle — she must be further down the inlet,' she called breathlessly.

Jenna enveloped the sobbing child in a blanket in the back of the Land Rover, and began rubbing her hair with a towel. At that moment, Andy's police SUV arrived with its lights flashing.

Ruaridh gave a shout. 'Look! There's a figure clinging to that rock, over there!'

They all followed the direction of his arm, and saw that there was indeed a human shape by a rock about fifty metres along from them. Jake and Ruaridh ran along the path, and Jenna saw Jake wade into the water. He reached for the woman, and hauled her towards the beach and out of the water. As Jake carried her back towards the car, Jenna could hear Gayle calling, 'Talli, my baby, where is she? Is she safe?'

Andy had hauled a blanket from the back of the police vehicle and wrapped it around the shivering woman, who was now weeping. The window of the Land Rover was slightly open, allowing Jenna to hear Gayle's tremor-filled words. 'Warren kept us on the island because there was a delivery due. I didn't realise he'd been here before, and had set up this whole racket. That man, Grant, was working for him here. Warren also paid him to get close to Talli, believing I wanted to take her away.' She turned anguished eyes to Jake. 'But it wasn't me! I wouldn't hurt my baby! I wanted to have her back with me, but I wouldn't go outside the law! I know she needs her daddy. I hope you realise that, Jake?'

Jake's face was grim as he nodded. Andy interrupted to say that the air ambulance would arrive within a few minutes.

Jake turned to Andy. 'We're taking Talli home to Ballintroon. My mother has called the doctor, and he's going to meet us there. Talli only had a brief ducking.'

As they sped off down the road, the helicopter swooped overhead on its way to collect Gayle and take her to hospital on the mainland. 'Will Gayle be all right?' Jenna whispered over Talli's head. The child was sleepy now that Jenna had whisked off her wet clothes and had dressed her in her own warm fleece, with a blanket round her.

'I think so — she was frightened, but perfectly coherent. Andy is arranging for a boat to go over to the island to investigate what was going on. But I suspect this was drugs related.'

Jenna lapsed into silence, cradling Talli in her arms.

Ailsa was waiting for them, along with Dr Drummond. Thanks to the generator, they could put Talli into a warm bath and give her a hot drink. After Ian had checked her over and declared her none the worse for her soaking, they put her to bed, where she slipped into a deep sleep holding Jake's hand.

Jenna stayed another night, and it

was a relief when the mains power came back on mid-morning. It was a bright, blustery day, with innocent-looking white clouds floating overhead. They had all slept much better, although Jake had been a bit cramped lying on Talli's bed cuddling her. She had woken a few times, but by morning was alert, though a little quiet. They telephoned the hospital on the mainland, and were told that Gayle was making a good recovery and would be released the next day. This clearly pleased Talli, who nodded and commented, 'Granny Gayle rescued me.'

Jake didn't like to question her too much, though he asked her where she and Gayle had slept the night before. 'In the car,' she'd replied solemnly. 'We had blankets and a pillow from the boat, and Granny Gayle wrapped me in her coat as well because I was cold. The car was shaking with the wind, but she told me we were safe, and that she'd bring me home to you in the morning. I knew you'd come and find us, Daddy.'

Her trusting eyes gazing at her father melted Jenna's heart.

Jake thought it would be best to take Talli's mind off the drama and encouraged her to have a session with her colouring book. Ailsa was also with them, scarcely able to take her eyes off her granddaughter, as if she would disappear if she did.

Jake was clearing up storm debris outside when Andy McCrinan's police vehicle rolled up. Jenna went out to join Jake and hear what the policeman had to say.

'Mrs. Hardiman seems to have no ill-effects, and Ian tells me that wee Talli is fine, I'm glad to hear.'

'She's a little subdued,' Jake said. 'We'll keep a watch on her to see if she has any psychological after-effects.'

Andy nodded. 'Children are surprisingly resilient, and I may have something to take her mind off it.'

'But what happened? Why were they on the islet?' Jenna prompted.

'Aye, of course you need to know.'

The policeman shoved his hands in the pockets of his waterproof jacket. 'When we reached the island we found Warren Hardiman and Grant Fenton shored up in Fenton's boat which he used for crab fishing. It was grounded out of reach of the sea, which is just as well. They made a run for it. We apprehended Fenton first and nabbed him, but unfortunately Hardiman slipped on the rocks and was swept out to sea. We picked him up about an hour later, but it was too late.'

There was a brief silence before Jake asked, frowning, 'What were they doing there — and why take Talli?'

'Fenton spilled the beans willingly once he was in custody. Hardiman originally visited Arasay to reconnoitre the place in order to develop a plan to snatch Talli and take her back to America. While he was here he had the idea that such a remote island would be just the place to smuggle drugs into the country. This was last February. He met Fenton who had just moved here and was looking for work. Hardiman set up the deliveries. Fenton also acquired the dog for the purpose of befriending Talli.'

Jake balled his fists. 'I knew he was up to no good.'

'It's been quite an operation. The man you found dead on the roadway back in March was one of the crew from a delivery ship — the conclusion was that he'd come to the village looking for a drink, and lost his way in the dark. An unfortunate accident, ironically. They were expecting a delivery yesterday, but they foolishly hadn't reckoned on the ferocity of the weather. That was their undoing — and the fact that his stepmother realised that there was something unlawful going on. She was apparently furious, and was berating him after they picked up Talli from the farm.'

'Gayle was always too outspoken for her own good,' Jake added grimly.

'Hardiman decided to try and keep her quiet for a day or two until the drugs were delivered, and he was going to leave with the boat while Fenton distributed the goods through their usual channels. But that meant taking Talli too. That was foolhardy, as they weren't prepared for a hostage situation. Mrs. Hardiman — she's a gutsy lady — saw the chance to escape when the men were out on the shore. She took the car keys and drove to the causeway. But she hadn't banked on the magnitude of the storm, and wasn't too good with a geared drive car. You saw the result of that.'

'And the causeway gave way,' Jenna added, shivering.

Jake put his arm round her, pulling her close, and asked Andy if he would like a coffee.

Andy smiled, the corners of his eyes crinkling as he looked into the sun. 'Aye, I will. You go ahead, as I have something to get from my car.'

Talli looked up as Jake and Jenna opened the door. She ran over to them, waving the picture she had been drawing. 'Look, Daddy, Auntie Jenna

— I've drawn a dog.'

They duly admired it, while Ailsa went to put on the kettle. Then they heard the front door opening, and Andy's footsteps in the corridor. His smiling face appeared round the doorway.

'I've got something — or someone — for Talli.'

Talli gave a squeal of delight. 'MacTavish!' The dog in Andy's arms began to squirm and whine with excitement, and as Talli reached for him, he licked her face, his stubby tail working frantically. She took him in her arms, giggling with delight, her happiness dissolving the tension of the past few days.

'Is he mine now?' she asked with wonder, looking hopefully into the policeman's face.

'Aye, he is that. Grant Fenton has to go away for a long time, and he won't be able to look after this little fella — so rather than him going to a rescue centre, I thought he would have a welcome home here. That is, if your daddy agrees?'

'Of course.' Jake's eyes were bright with love for his daughter, and Jenna felt her heart melt totally as he turned to her. 'And I think Jenna agrees too. That just about makes our family complete.'

They looked into each other's eyes and smiled.

We do hope that you have enjoyed reading this large print book.

Did you know that all of our titles are available for purchase?

We publish a wide range of high quality large print books including:
Romances, Mysteries, Classics
General Fiction
Non Fiction and Westerns

Special interest titles available in large print are:
The Little Oxford Dictionary
Music Book, Song Book
Hymn Book, Service Book

Also available from us courtesy of Oxford University Press:
Young Readers' Dictionary
(large print edition)
Young Readers' Thesaurus
(large print edition)

For further information or a free brochure, please contact us at:
Ulverscroft Large Print Books Ltd.,
The Green, Bradgate Road, Anstey,
Leicester, LE7 7FU, England.
Tel: (00 44) 0116 236 4325
Fax: (00 44) 0116 234 0205

Other titles in the
Linford Romance Library:

NEW YEAR NEW GUY

Angela Britnell

When Polly organises a surprise reunion for her fiancé and his long-lost American friend, her sister, Laura, grudgingly agrees to help keep the secret. And when the plain-spoken, larger-than-life Hunter McQueen steps off the bus in her rainy Devon town and only just squeezes into her tiny car, it confirms that Laura has made a big mistake in going along with her sister's crazy plan. But could the tall, handsome man with the Nashville drawl be just what Laura needs to shake up her life and start something new?